Paisley Memories

The Beginning of Me

Zelle Andrews

Zelle Andrews

Published by:
Southern Yellow Pine (SYP) Publishing
4351 Natural Bridge Rd.
Tallahassee, FL 32305

www.syppublishing.com

This is a work of fiction. Names, characters, places, and events that occur either are the products of the author's imagination or are used fictitiously. Any resemblance to actual persons, places, or events is purely coincidental.

The contents and opinions expressed in this book do not necessarily reflect the views and opinions of Southern Yellow Pine Publishing, nor does the mention of brands or trade names constitute endorsement.

ISBN-10: 1940869544
ISBN-13: 978-1-940869-54-4
ISBN-13: ePub 978-1-940869-55-1
ISBN-13: Adobe eBook 978-1-940869-56-8
Library of Congress Control Number: 2015952849

Printed in the United States of America
First Edition
November 2015

ACKNOWLEDGEMENTS

This story started on a scrap of paper on the kitchen counter. My husband found it when cleaning. I was embarrassed and yanked it away. He had no idea I was working on a novel, but he has been encouraging me since.

Shortly after that, I joined Tallahassee Writers Association, and I haven't looked back. I came away from the first meeting with my head spinning, but also with a goal. I was going to be an author!

Many people played a huge part in making this dream come true. My critique group, The Outcasts: Elizabeth Babski, Jayne Wallace, Robert Frink, and Jeff Bauer. You people are amazing, talented writers. Without your guidance, I'd still be floundering.

Kimberley Baldwin, who requested my most coveted cookie recipe as a form of payment for being my beta reader. You rock!

To my initial editor, Becky Stephens. Thank you for your professionalism and patience with a new author.

Rob Andrews, my husband. You have been amazing for the last four years. You took my endeavor serious and pushed me to completion.

To my daughter, Sarah, my sidekick at book launches, parties, and book events. You inspire me.

To my son, Dylan, who came to my aid during many technical computer difficulties. Your unending patience is appreciated more than you know.

To the Wakulla Historical Society staff. I came in unannounced one day because I was having issues with the timeline festivals in Wakulla County and other historical events. Several people dropped what they were doing and gave my husband and me their undivided attention and shared their stories. It just made me love Wakulla County even more. Thank you.

Whew. It is done. Without all of you, and many more, this book would still be swirling around in my head. Now, I have room for the next story.

Dedication

I dedicate this book to my children, Sarah and Dylan. Through many years of laughter and tears, these two beautiful souls have enriched my life more than they could possibly know.

PROLOGUE

The weight of Paisley on my hip caused my high heels to sink slowly in the soft, Alabama red clay. Many people came to pay their respects. They lingered for a while, hugging and consoling each other, but when the first one decided to leave, the rest followed like a stampede. Potted mums were removed and placed to the side. The uncomfortable, gray metal chairs were folded and placed in a waiting truck to be returned to the funeral home. I held my breath as they lowered my dad's casket into his new home. With each inch the casket descended in its red tomb, my heart descended too.

The last guest reached out to touch my shoulder as she shook her head. No words came to her. I didn't even know who she was. She drove away without saying a word. Everyone left, but their whispers lingered and became a dark, oppressive cloud—whispers of what would become of my daughter Paisley and me, now that my dad had died. The sting of their words still circulated: out of wedlock, orphan, retarded, unemployed, uneducated, high school dropout. I blinked to stop the tears flowing from my eyes and stood in silence as clay was dropped on top of his casket. The funeral director attempted to persuade me to leave, but it didn't work. I had to see this. The grave digger placed a large mountain of red clay over the grave that made me think of a gigantic ant bed. He patted it down, reminding me of patting someone's back when saying good-bye. Well, this was good-bye.

When the last person left, I pulled my heels free from their clay prison, heaved Paisley a little higher on my hip, and walked to the headstone. Without a thought, I raked my hand over the engraving of George Daniel Cooper and Margaret Rose Cooper. My mom's engraved date of death only three days after my birth was green with algae and smooth to the touch. My dad's date of death, April 5, 2013, felt new, rough, and sharp on my fingertips.

"I hate you," I said as my fingertips lingered on his name. Then my fingers curled into an ugly claw. I walked toward my dad's 1957 Thunderbird, my escape from this place, and fastened Paisley in her car seat.

The Samsonite luggage was stacked so high it bulged under the dry-rotted convertible top. Duct tape covered a previous rip from when our neighbor's overweight cat decided it was a nice spot to catch a few rays. It was the only waterproof part of the top.

His car, which was now mine, rattled to a start. After making sure I was alone, off came the depressing black dress. My high heels were next. There I sat, in my cutoff jeans, gray tank top, jade-colored toenails, and flip flops on the floorboards. The house was already sold, so the only place to change would have been in a fast-food stop. I didn't want to stop anywhere on the way out of town. I just wanted to get the "heck out of Dodge." So done with this town and the people in it. The gears moaned in protest when I lowered the ragtop.

A few memories of my life here traveled with me: Paisley, in the car seat beside me, my dad's lucky wheat penny in my pocket, and the family album I grabbed on the way out the door. Dad always said that family albums should be filled with treasured photos of fond memories. I stopped putting pictures in it when Dad died. There wasn't even a photo of Paisley, and she was a little over a year old.

While driving through the iron-gated entrance of Goodbread Memory Gardens in Brooksville, Alabama, I

2

purposely knocked the rearview and side mirrors out of place, so I wasn't tempted to look back. Someone once told me not to look back when leaving for a journey, as it was bad luck. I'd had all the bad luck one person could stand in this life, and I wasn't going to take any chances. This was going to be a journey of epic proportions.

CHAPTER ONE

We had been on the road a little over a year, going in circles from town to town throughout Georgia and Northern Florida. Funny…when you think about all the traveling we did and we were only a few hours away from where we started. Our clothes were as worn out as my patience. Paisley had grown like kudzu. Each month, we hit the yard sales just to get her clothing that fit. Yard sales are the way to go when you have a baby. I guess all two-year-olds grow fast.

We were in the southern, deep-fried town of Crawfordville, Florida. A place where old boiled peanuts go to die. A tractor was parked half off the highway, with grass a foot high around the wheels. The sun was setting, and after the long drive, food and a bed were exactly what we needed. A big sigh escaped my lips when I pulled up to a drive-thru. I hoped their food was better than the scenery.

"Two cheeseburgers, two fries, a Pepsi, and a carton of milk, please."

Dad's car grumbled, and the engine stalled. I slammed my head into the back of the headrest, but that didn't fix it. After four turns of the key and pumps of the gas pedal, not unlike a vintage Singer sewing machine, it turned over. This piece of junk needed work, and so did I. We were a perfect match, much better than Thom and me.

Thom Perkins, a guy I'd known since my booger-picking kindergarten days, hit his peak of cuteness in high school. In the twelfth grade, he used to strut down the corridors at school in his skinny jeans, singing "Glad You Came" by The Wanted. The day I saw him flirting with Monica Simmons—a little, boney, fly-back, blonde-haired girl who stuffed her bra—my hormones kicked into gear and I decided he had to be mine. *What a mistake*, I thought, and shook my head as I tried to refocus.

Paisley slept peacefully beside me in her car seat, tucked tightly in the faded, green paisley blanket she came home from the hospital in.

Through the grimy, drive-thru window, I saw the teenaged, fast-food employee flirting with a boy. My order dangled in her hand. I quickly rapped on the window with my knuckles, but immediately retracted my hand. I rubbed my knuckles on my shorts to remove the Ebola and Salmonella viruses I was sure lingered on them.

She sauntered over and bumped the padded lever at her hip to open the window.

"I'm sorry, ma'am," she said, while looking over her shoulder at the boy. She turned to face me. "Would you like some condoms with this?"

The boy bent over with laughter.

"No, I do not want condoms with this, but I will take some ketchup," I replied through gritted teeth.

"What?" she asked with the classic deer in the headlights look. The color drained from her face as she realized what she'd said. She shoved a fistful of ketchup packets in the bag, crushed it closed, and handed it to me red-faced. Forcing a smile, I handed her money, to the penny, and pulled away. My sense of humor was shot. Having a baby does that to you. First, you lose your figure and then your sense of humor. As a matter of fact, I was sure of it. I guess when we push the baby out that gets pushed out too. Good-bye sense of humor, hello baby! Yep, life as I knew it was over.

Several fat raindrops hit the windshield as I pulled away from the drive-thru. A few more followed, reminding me of popcorn kernels blowing up in the microwave. The blades were ancient, but I took a chance and turned the windshield wipers on. Water smeared across the window. The wipers didn't work with bugs or with fat raindrops. After three sporadic swishes, one of the rubber pieces came partially off the metal bar and flapped back and forth like a seal's flipper.

"Great. Now I need to replace the blades," I mumbled.

I drove across the street to the brightly lit, twenty-four-hour, do-it-yourself car wash and parked under the rusted overhang. Taking that old blade off to fix it wasn't easy. When I gave the wiper a test run, it made a horrible screeching sound as it dragged across the glass. I turned the wipers off and sat there a minute, trying to collect my thoughts and subdue my anger. *Tomorrow. I could deal with it tomorrow*, I thought. The rain increased, coming down in sheets. *Please, just stop raining, already.* Tomorrow I would try to find a hardware store employee who was bored out of his mind, who might take pity on a young, single mom and put new ones on for me.

The smell of the cheeseburger and fries was intoxicating, and the parking lot was as good a place as any to eat before they got cold. Static was on most stations, but eventually one came in clear enough to stop and listen. An eighties classic came through the speakers. Madonna belted, "I'm Keeping My Baby." Paisley sighed and so did I. Within less than a minute, I guzzled my soda and was half-finished with my greasy burger and fries when Paisley opened her eyes and smiled. The side of her face was damp with perspiration, and her black hair was matted and stuck to the side of her cheek. I wiped away the sweat, using the corner of her blanket as a bib.

"You always wake up happy, don't you? Do you ever have a bad day?"

She looked at me, smiled, and kicked her feet. She raised her roly-poly arms to me. Shoving the last bite of cheeseburger in my mouth, I unbuckled her car seat and let her escape into my lap. She went right for my purse, as always, and pulled out

7

her sippy cup. She gnawed the French fries and ripped the cheeseburger apart, barely giving me time to fill her sippy cup with milk.

It was time to find a place to sleep…and Paisley needed a bath. I read somewhere once that you need to talk to your children even if they aren't talking yet. It connects those snappy things in their heads, or something like that. I'd already told Paisley so much trash about my life, it's a good thing she couldn't talk yet. She got an earful about Thom too.

Twenty minutes later, we parked in a motel parking lot. After loading up all my worldly belongings, I managed to get Paisley on my hip and waddled to the front door.

Though the motel appeared to be only one step up from a homeless shelter we had stayed in one night, it was inviting after our long travel. I imagined myself soaking in a hot bath with bubbles peaked so high they tickled my nose. I wouldn't surface until I was certified a raisin and, then I would collapse into a coma for a week.

Reality hit me. Who was I kidding? I hadn't had a good night's sleep in months. Not with Paisley with me. Sometimes we took naps in the car. I could say with no uncertainty that old, dried-out vinyl does not compare to my bed at home in the slightest. On the nights I splurged so we could get a hot shower, I always looked for the cheapest motel. Forget Motel 6. I'd settle for Motel 3, hoping it was half the price. From the looks of the place, I thought we'd found it.

The clerk behind the counter stared at Paisley and anger began to build up inside me. Why do people have to make it obvious they are staring at her? *Jerk.* "Let it go, Tess. Just let it go," I mumbled. He probably can't see well anyway with those glasses. His eyes magnified almost two times their normal size when he looked up. He resembled the little old men who greet you at discount stores.

As I approached the counter, I thought he was chewing gum. I was mistaken. He stuck his two fingers in his mouth and

8

adjusted his dentures. "Dear God, please remind me to brush and floss every day," I whispered.

I plopped Paisley's diapered butt down on the countertop, with her facing me as I dug in my purse for my wallet. "How much is a single bed?"

The man cleared his throat to get my attention, and Paisley presented me with roses, beautiful roses. They looked exactly identical to the ones...oh, no! They *were* the exact ones. The very roses that, seconds ago, were meticulously arranged in a blue and white ceramic vase on the counter. Baby's breath dangled from the rim of the vase, with water droplets on the counter and down her pants. She clutched four of the dozen yellow roses in her fists, barely missing the sharp thorns just above her fingers. The other eight roses resembled pixie sticks on the floor. One poke from those thorns and I knew the entire motel would vacate out the emergency exits, thinking it was the fire alarm. *Bait and switch*, I thought. *Do the bait and switch, and there won't be a scene.*

"Oh, look Paisley. It's piggy." I grabbed her favorite toy, a rubber pig from my purse. She spied it and released the flowers instantly to take her beloved pig. I caught the falling roses, thorns and all. My eyes instinctively closed to the pain. When I opened them, I silently rearranged the roses in the vase that remained on the counter, jamming in the baby's breath. Why would a cheap motel splurge on expensive roses? Wouldn't plastic have been more their league?

"That will be forty-five dollars, ma'am."

He mumbled in irritation under his breath as we exchanged cash for keys. Paisley and I headed down the long corridor to our room. As I approached our room, the door beside ours was jerked open. Before me was a man, five feet, eight inches tall who resembled a pot-bellied pig. His dingy, white tank top was riding up on his protruding, hairy belly. The stench from the cigar wedged in the corner of his mouth almost made me gag. Thin wisps of hair, which had been combed up and over from a

9

part that was a mere inch above his left ear, clung to his scalp. Suspenders drooped around his hips over a pair of black slacks that hung over mismatched socks, no shoes.

"That's it," he yelled back into the room. "I'm done. I don't know why I keep you around." His eyes fixed on me and then on Paisley. "I'd get more conversation from this lady's baby." He studied Paisley for a minute more, and I could tell he was second-guessing his statement.

He spit at my feet and yelled over his shoulder. "Be in the car in fifteen minutes, or your ass is on its own!" He brushed past me and Paisley.

I tried to scurry by the room without looking in, but I couldn't help myself. She looked about as worn out as I felt. Her dark hair hung in a greasy mess over her shoulders. I assumed he ate her food too, because she looked too skinny. A half-packed suitcase, with wrinkled clothes thrown in carelessly, was laid open in front of her on the bed. Despite her worn-out appearance, she still had spunk.

"Can I help you?" she asked defensively, her hand on her hip.

"Nope," I answered. I hurried by with Paisley and our luggage in tow. There was a bright side to all of this; my life could be her life. I shuddered at the thought.

"Motel, sweet motel," I said and turned the key to our overnight home and put Paisley down on the carpeted floor. Paisley crawled to the nearest wall, stood bracing herself with her hands, and cruised around holding onto the wall. It reminded me of when I was learning to skate at the skating rink. The day she learned to walk would be awesome, if she ever learned to walk. After the door was locked, I wedged a chair under the handle for good measure. I didn't want my daughter's face on a milk carton due to my carelessness.

I grabbed the small travel bag out of my suitcase and took Paisley into the bathroom to give her a bath. When I pulled back

10

the shower curtain, a small white mouse jumped out of the folds and scampered across my feet.

Paisley didn't know what to think of me standing on the toilet, screaming at the top of my lungs. When she began to scream, the guy in the next room banged on the wall and told us to both shut up.

I did as he ordered and tried to calm Paisley while being on mouse lookout. A small strip of duct tape was in the tub. I reached in and peeled back the corner to reveal a crack in the plastic liner. To think! I had always believed Alabamians were the kings of rednecks. I stood corrected. Did all men use duct tape to repair everything? I knew for certain it did not repair everything.

The old man at the front desk didn't seem surprised when I told him about the mouse and duct tape. He hesitated when I asked for another room.

"Did you use the toilet? If you used the toilet, we will have to charge you for two rooms."

"Only to stand on when I was screaming at the mouse," I answered. It took us another thirty minutes to get settled in another room, after I did a thorough mouse and duct tape inspection.

The last things I remembered, as Paisley snuggled close to me with the scent of her sweaty hair, were the exfoliating texture of the twenty-five thread count sheet on our bed as I pulled it up, and hoping the chair wedged under the loose doorknob would hold.

CHAPTER TWO

I dreamed the best dream I've had in a long time. Sand was below me and the sunshine above…sand so white I was convinced I'd fallen into a bag of sugar. Dad and I couldn't afford vacations. It wasn't "within our budget" was his famous quote. I really wanted this dream to be awesome. I squirted suntan lotion on my hands and rubbed it on my legs. My legs weren't as jiggly as they normally were. They felt different. I raised my designer sunglasses up, the kind I could afford in a dream, and glimpsed down at my legs. They were toned, skinny, and tanned, and I was wearing a bikini. Not just any bikini, but a hot pink, pleather bikini. This dream was going to get milked for all it was worth. No more baby fat on me. I'd heard that after your baby fat is a year old, you can't claim it as baby fat. Being past the one-year mark officially makes it *my* fat—except in this awesome dream.

Seagulls jumped around on the shore, grabbing morsels of snacks as they washed in with each wave. It was entertaining…for about a millisecond.

A speck on the beach began to emerge in the distance. A few seconds later, the speck sprouted arms and legs—very muscular arms and legs. Chiseled muscles covered his body. His boobs were bigger than mine and flexed with each step he took closer to me. I don't know how guys do that, but I enjoyed it. Sandy blond hair and pearly white teeth were coming at me. His dark green, jet-set trunks hung precariously from his hipbones. Well, looky there…he has my name with a flaming heart around it tattooed on his chest.

Another second later he stood in front of me, dripping wet, with sand stuck to his tanned calves and feet. I've never seen sand look sexy. His green eyes resembled marbles with swirls in them. He spoke a foreign language I couldn't understand, but really, who cares what he said. He was eye candy. He gently took my trembling hand in his warm ones and steered me closer to the water's edge. The sound of the surf was too loud for me to understand what he said. He tried again to tell me something, and I couldn't quite make it out. I leaned in closer to his full, pouty lips and felt his warm breath on my face. He screamed in my ear, in perfect English, with no accent, "Wake up! Paisley is flushing the toilet!"

The sound of the toilet flushing made me bolt upright in bed. Cold water splashed over my toes when I crossed the bathroom threshold. Paisley somehow managed to clog the toilet, and water was flowing out geyser-style. Before I could reach her, she flushed it again. Barely visible was the corner of a washcloth sticking out of the toilet bowl opening.

I lunged for it and yanked it out, just as the water funneled down once more. I reached behind the base and turned the water off. Paisley watched me as I threw all the bathroom towels down on the floor. At that precise moment, I made an executive decision that we would be leaving early. As a matter of fact, we would be leaving within the next few minutes. I closed the porcelain lid, plopped down, and stared at Paisley.

"Why'd you do this?" Oblivious to my question, she balanced herself with the support of one hand on the side of the tub. Were other parents dealing with the same thing? She looked at me with her slanted eyes, grabbed a wet towel from the floor, and wiped her face. She was trying to give herself the bath I forgot to give her.

I must have wrung those towels out twenty times each, trying to get the water off the floor. I'll bet the cleaning lady never got the floor as clean as I did. With no more clean washcloths, I used one of my clean socks to give Paisley a sponge bath. Our bags were packed, and we were dressed in record time as we headed for check-out five hours early.

As I handed over the room key, a woman behind me at the check-out counter tapped her foot impatiently. Standing there in her black silk pajamas, her hair a matted mess, and old makeup on her face, she looked ready to explode. She slammed her fist on the counter and yelled as I ran out the door. She screamed about water seeping through the ceiling, ruining her Balenciaga purse and demanded the motel pay for it, in addition to emotional suffering from the condition of the yellow roses delivered from her husband. Then there was something about missing their anniversary...car broke down...suing. I couldn't get to my car fast enough.

"Way to go, Paisley. Way to go. Just keep messing up my life," I mumbled.

The sun was just starting to peek through the pine trees as I loaded her in the car with my luggage. I don't know how long we sat in the car with the engine running. I wasn't sure where to go from there. Eventually, Paisley fell asleep again.

How did we get here? How did I get here? Not this town, but at this place in my life. We were doing nothing but living the life of gypsies wandering from here to there.

Remember, Tess, you have a choice. My choice sat on the dashboard. It was the pamphlet that a little, old-lady volunteer handed me at the shelter. I don't know why I still had it. Just wasn't sure what to do, I guess. This was the fifth time I looked at it. "You Have Choices" stood out in bold print on the cover. Dedicated professionals were listed who would jump at the chance to take a baby and give it to someone else. The thing is, I knew someone else might be just what Paisley needed. I read it from cover to cover and kept focusing on the last few words, "best decision for the child." It wasn't until Paisley moved that I

14

saw I had twisted the pamphlet in my hand. I shoved it in my purse. Out of sight, out of mind.

Our next stop was Myra Jean's restaurant just down the highway. I ordered the cheapest meal on the menu. The waitress watched me while she poured my coffee, hesitated a second, and then placed the coffee pot on the table. She patted me on the shoulder as she walked away.

Paisley's head rotated in the manner of an owl watching its prey. She made eye contact with each and every customer and squealed at each one, making them laugh. I, on the other hand, didn't find it funny, not one bit. She shredded her napkin into itty-bitty pieces within a matter of seconds, and popped them in her mouth. I took a chance with *Jaws* and fished them out. All napkins were moved out of her reach. She kicked off her sandals and managed to stick her big toe in her mouth. Instant gratification for her, but it drove me crazy. Thank God for highchairs with straps. Otherwise I'd never get to eat.

"Toes make great appetizers, don't they?" the waitress said to Paisley as she placed our breakfast on the table. Paisley could give a professional contortionist a run for her money. I tried everything short of a full-body cast to get her to stop. One day gravity would affect those feet, and she wouldn't be able to lift them anymore.

"You can't walk on your butt cheeks. Put your feet down." I tried to gently pull her feet from her mouth. The screech she emitted caused the people in the next booth to jump.

"Temporary win for you, little girl," I whispered as I leaned across the table. She shoved one calloused toe back into her mouth as I plopped a wad of butter on my grits.

It slowly dissolved, sliding down the sides of my mound of grits. It reminded me of lava flowing down a volcano. I grabbed a piece of bacon, dipped it in the buttery grits, and shoved the entire piece in my mouth. So greasy, and good. Very close to the taste of a home-cooked meal. I missed those. I hadn't eaten one of those in months. This meal was going to be savored, bite by bite. In between Paisley exchanging toes, I got a few mouthfuls of grits and scrambled eggs in her.

People on the other side of the restaurant began to sing "Happy Birthday," followed by the customary applause.

A little girl, about seven years old, dashed by my table. She stopped so abruptly her long, blonde pigtails smacked her in the face. "I found someone," she hollered. "Ma'am, would you take our picture? It's G-mom's birthday. She's ninety-five years old."

When I opened my mouth to decline, she shoved a camera in my hand. I pulled Paisley's highchair around with me and watched as people all rushed to squeeze close together. The group was much larger than I thought. There must have been over thirty people who showed up for this G-mom's birthday bash. She could still bring it.

It had been a while since I held a camera. The last time was in an elective class at high school. Taking photographs for the yearbook was awesome—just about the only class I made an A in all year. I gave the camera a once-over to reacquaint myself with the buttons and then gave instructions to the group.

"Everyone who's tall, please stand in the back; people in the middle, slightly turn to face each other; and all others turn to face the one in front of you. All kids in the front, and the birthday girl front and center." They scurried for a moment with moms doing a quick spit clean of their kids' faces, and I repositioned the grandchildren so they sat or squatted in a semi-circle around their grandmother. "Okay, guys, act as if you love each other." Too many people wore stiff smiles. "Say, Tess's meal is free," I said with an exaggerated smile. Everyone laughed as I shot about six quick photos.

"I'll bet she took a great one of Uncle Henry," one woman said. "Even Aunt Gladys smiled. I haven't seen her smile in months since her pet raccoon died last year. Hopefully, she held the camera at an angle and made my triple chin a double." Loud laughter followed her deprecating comment.

"Are you a photographer?" she asked.

"No, I just took photos for my yearbook in school," I replied.

After thanking me, the woman took the camera from my hands and took a few more random shots. I scooted the highchair back to our table, and when I sat down, she was standing next to me. She lowered her tortoiseshell glasses and assessed us. Her eyes locked onto mine for a moment, and she sat down beside Paisley. The situation suddenly became awkward.

"Are you new in town? You don't look familiar."

Taking a deep breath, I answered, "Yes, we are. We are just passing through."

"From what I've seen here, I think you know how to get people to relax for a photo. You have some natural talent," she said.

She looked down at Paisley sucking her toe again as the waitress slid the bill on the counter.

"I'll tell you what. I'll pay for your breakfast if you come to my house." She picked up the receipt and waved it in the air as if enticing me to say yes. "I just might have an easy photo project. Traveling folks always need extra cash, right?" she added with a smile.

I studied her face for a moment and looked at Paisley. I'd heard about these small town serial killers in the news all the time. They prey on helpless victims such as me. If I'd taken those three, free, kickboxing classes I'd won on the radio station a few years ago, I might be able to fight her off. We could be dealing with a Florida chainsaw massacre here with Granny as the ring leader. She could butcher us both into tiny pieces and take pictures with the very camera I just used. She's trying to lure me to her Hansel and Gretel cottage in the Florida swamps, and since Paisley was small, she would sell her to the circus. Geez, I really need to stop watching those late night horror movies at the motels.

17

I glanced at Paisley and thought of the few dollars I had left. If she paid enough, maybe I could stay a short while and look for a temporary job. I mean, really, would a serial killer attend a grandmother's ninety-fifth birthday party? It's amazing how the offer of money can dilute the danger of a situation.

"Where do you live?" I whispered in defeat.

"Just twenty miles from here. I'll give you directions." She jotted it down then paid my bill and hers. The tables they'd occupied looked like a trash dumpster. As much as I needed a job right now, I was thankful I wasn't a waitress at Myra Jean's. Bless their hearts.

The note card had directions on it, directions to a paying job. While brushing dried grits from Paisley's face, I mumbled, "What have I done?"

CHAPTER THREE

Thirty minutes. What could I find to do in a strange town for thirty minutes? I didn't know what I was supposed to be taking photos of. She better not be expecting me to take nudie photos. I cringed at the thought.

Across the street was a car parts store. With just enough time to get my windshield wiper checked out, I pulled up in the parking lot.

The mechanic straddled a wine barrel that was sawed in half, turned upside down, and used as a chair. He dropped his cigarette, extinguished it with the heel of his alligator boot, and walked toward my car. His long, black hair, braided in a plait down his back, had gray strands dotting his temples. Subtlety was not one of his strong characteristics as he eyeballed me the same as a five-year-old child does a melting ice cream cone. I rolled my window down to talk to him.

"Are you new here, missy?"

I bristled. "My name is Tess, and yes, I am new here." Dirk was the name embroidered on his work shirt. Who names their kid Dirk? I could see it all. He's in elementary school on the playground in the sandbox, and the kids start teasing him because they can't pronounce it. They start calling him Dirt. He beat them all to a pulp and was labeled a problem child. All future job prospects doomed. I would have begged my dad to change my name.

He looked at me with squinted eyes to block out the morning sun.

"What can I do for you?"

I pointed toward my windshield wiper. "My rubber thingy came loose."

He raised an eyebrow and shook his head. "I hate it when rubber thingy's come loose," he teased. "It's happened to me a couple of times. I'll be right back."

Okay, Dirk. I'll just be right here. Medusa stared back at me through the mirror of my visor. The charcoal color under my eyes went perfectly with my black, tangled hair. No wonder the waitress left the entire coffee pot for me. There was just enough time for me to run my fingers through my hair and pull it back in a clip before Dirk reappeared.

"Last rubber thingy on the shelf," he said. "It's your lucky day." He took off both the old ones and replaced them with the new ones. "That'll be nineteen dollars and ninety-eight cents, Tess."

"Wh-What?" I asked, flabbergasted.

"The blades are nineteen ninety-eight for the pair. I knocked off the tax since you're new in town." He winked and gave me a crooked smile.

"Don't you have a cheaper pair?"

"This is the *only* pair."

In desperation, I pleaded, "Can I just buy one blade and pay half price? The other one still sort of worked. You can just put it back on."

"Can't do that, Tess. They come in a package."

"But I need one, not two," I whined. I couldn't believe I was getting ripped off in this one-traffic-light town. My chest constricted. Panic started to kick in, and I actually thought of racing off in my car. But jail didn't sound too appealing. My mug shot in the news, someone from Alabama comes down and recognizes it. Petty theft, it would say. And because inquiring minds wanted to know, they would dig deeper and find out I stole wiper blades. I could feel the shame already.

20

"But, if you bring yourself down a notch and don't get wound up about me calling you missy, I'll let them go for free," he said.

What a jerk. Before I was able to make a decision, he lifted the hood.

"What are you doing now?"

"Don't worry. It's free," he answered. Once he checked the oil, he slammed the hood down. Yellow paint flakes fell off on impact.

"It all looks good. Do you plan on fixing her up?" he asked as he leaned on the hood. "I'm the best mechanic in town. Body work is my specialty."

"I don't think I could afford you," I quipped. We stood staring at each other for an awkward moment of silence.

"That'll be nineteen ninety-eight. I'll let you slide on the tax."

He smiled, and I noticed he was missing an eyetooth. It was probably punched out from the last person he sold wipers to.

I handed him a twenty-dollar bill and got back in the car. I didn't care about getting my two pennies. I just wanted to leave.

"Take care of this babe. She's a classic," he said and slapped her on the hood as a farewell. More yellow paint chips fell. "Have a great day, missy."

I hate that name. I know it's just a southern thing equivalent to sweetie, sugar, honey, and dumplin', but I still hate it just the same. Sometimes I'm not sweet, I ain't made of sugar or honey, and I'm not floating in chicken broth.

I watched as he sauntered back to the store and plopped his greasy-assed jeans down on the wine barrel again. He smiled and waved good-bye as if giving me permission to leave. I pouted half the way to the serial killer's house.

***

21

The drive was much longer than she said. I'm sure it's because I was going at the speed of a sloth down a sandy washer-board road. Salty air filled the car as I unrolled the windows. I said "ah," letting it out for a long time to hear my voice vibrate from the rutted road. Paisley stared wide-eyed and mesmerized by the new sound I made. She opened her mouth and made the same sound. We "ahhed," all the way there.

Wild palms scattered along the roadside, some as large as trees. A white bird stretched its neck while wading in a puddle in a marshy area on the side of the road. As I drove closer, the bird stretched its wings as if to take flight. For one fleeting moment, I thought it resembled a stork and sped up a little faster to leave it behind. A stork caught up with me once, and that was enough.

Fresh, salty air cleansed my mind of stress. The trees and shrubbery thinned as we came closer to the coast. Old, weathered cypress stumps dotted the beach. This was the first time I'd ever seen the beach. Alabama wasn't too far away, but we just never made the time.

Paisley reached toward the open window as the wind hit her hand. Her giggles filled the car. Pretty soon I was doing the same thing, but moving my hand back and forth like an ocean wave. Paisley tried to mimic me. She flipped her hand back and forth at the wrist. The sound of my laughter startled me. I had completely forgotten the sound of it. It had been so long since I last laughed.

I was still smiling when a mailbox appeared, just as the woman described it. It was a dolphin made of concrete. The flippers that held the mailbox reminded me of a butler holding a serving tray.

"Now, there is something you don't see every day."

I parked the car next to a beat-up SUV. The house was adorable for being built in the 1950s. Bright yellow, real-plank siding with white trim, covered with a silver tin roof. Conch shells of various sizes lined the weathered railing of the front porch. Broken seashells littered the raised flowerbeds which grew nothing but sandspurs. Two old, wooden rockers invited visitors to sit for a while. Warm beach sand covered my flip flops when my feet hit the ground. I had time to relish the moment for a second before Paisley ruined it. Her big toe was in her mouth again.

"Glad you made it. Welcome to Panacea."

The woman wore faded denim capris, a bright green T-shirt with cartoonish-looking creatures on it, and balanced on her head was an oversized beach hat that flapped in the breeze. "Ain't it a beautiful day?" She smiled, holding onto the brim of her hat to keep it from blowing away.

I smiled in agreement and pulled Paisley from the car. A gust of wind twisted and turned her hair into a mini tornado at her scalp.

"You live here…on the beach?"

"Yes, with my niece. She owns the house but is away on business. It will be just the three of us. I could never afford something as nice as this on the salary of a freelance photographer. I would have gone with her, but I didn't want to miss the party at Myra Jean's. And someone had to take care of the chickens." She winked at me.

"Chickens? You mean cluck, cluck, covered in feathers, egg-laying chickens?"

"Yep. Beachfront eggs instead of backyard eggs every morning. Do you want to see them?"

Never was a good time for me. "Maybe later." A view of the sandy, white beach caught my eye. Now, where was that tattooed man of my dreams?

She pivoted on her bare toes and headed for the house. "Come on in."

"Yes, ma'am."

She whirled around suddenly, "Uh uh. You can leave that 'ma'am' stuff in whatever town you came from. My name is

Naomi. Naomi Mitchell. If I really take a liking to you, I'll let you call me Butterball. All my friends do."

Butterball walked up the cobblestone path to the house with Paisley and me not too far behind. She wiped her feet on the braided welcome mat, and I copied her even though nothing was on my shoes. What a fishbowl of a house it was, windows from one end of the house to the other with nothing but the sky and the Gulf farther down the dunes for a view. I was a puppy on display in a store window, when I noticed she didn't have curtains on the windows.

"Don't you worry about privacy without curtains?"

"Nah. Who'd want to look at ole Butterball? Besides, we're too high up on the dunes for anyone to look in. Unless it's the paparazzi, of course, but I haven't done anything to make me famous...lately."

Paisley freed herself from my grasp and crawled to the window facing the Gulf. She fastened her hands suction cup style, smashing her nose against the pane. She was as mesmerized as I was.

"Make yourself at home. I need to get a few things so we can go over the photo project," she said as she vanished into the back of the house.

Despite my feeling of being exposed to the world by all the windows, the rest of the décor was warm and cozy. Warm, burnt-orange-colored tiles covered the floor. Two oversized chairs and a worn, denim-covered couch faced a massive fireplace. The mantel was made of an old barn beam, weathered with age. Built-in bookcases made of walnut held an assortment of novels and mementos surrounding the fireplace.

Curiosity got the best of me and I tiptoed over to the bookcase. Her variety of genres went from Jean Auel's *Clan of the Cave Bear* to *Gone with the Wind* by Margaret Mitchell. Many books on archaeology and prehistoric Florida lined the shelves. The ones with the most wear and tear must have been Butterball's niece's favorites.

24

I browsed the small library of books and noticed the fireplace was one huge piece of limestone with fossilized remains of ancient seashells, some still imbedded, and others just the impression of what once lived millions of years ago. A dark object slightly protruding from the limestone caught my eye. The dull, black, ridged object came to a sharp point. It was a shark tooth—not just any shark tooth, but one the size of a dinner plate. I couldn't fathom how large that sea creature must have been in these Florida waters.

If this photo gig didn't work out I could always chisel it from its home, of probably a million years, and hawk it at the nearest pawn shop.

"Isn't that the coolest thing you ever did see?" Butterball asked.

I nodded but couldn't meet her eyes because of what I had thought of doing.

"The limestone came from a local quarry. Check out the meg tooth in there." She pointed to the black object. "My niece is good friends with the guy who owns the quarry, and they almost crushed it to use for filler in the road when she fell in love with it. She purchased it on the spot. It must weigh more than my SUV. Did you see the meg tooth?" She walked to the spot where I contemplated thievery. "Megaladon was a giant prehistoric shark that lived millions of years ago. They could grow to about half the width of a football field. No enemies and ate anything stupid enough to swim by. Mafia of the water." Butterball smiled to herself as if impressed with her knowledge.

The life of a meg sounded pretty good, to have no enemies and be able to eat whomever I didn't like. Yep, I wanted to be a meg and eat all those people in high school in Alabama and take a big chunk out of Thom's ass.

"Sorry about the history lesson. I guess my niece's talking has rubbed off on me." She laughed. "Come on in the kitchen, and I'll show you what I have."

I stole one more look at the treasure partially buried in limestone, saw Paisley was still glued to the window, and moved to see what Butterball had in store for me. An assortment of photographs covered an old butcher block counter.

Some photos were of children rock climbing, others of food vendors, jewelry stands, cotton-candied faces, spectators at parades. One picture showed a child holding what appeared to be cooked, brown spaghetti. I saw a familiar face looking back at me. I tapped my finger on the photo, and before I could ask, she answered.

"That's Dirk Ramsey, our local mechanic."

"I met him this morning," I said grim-faced. "He tried to charge me a butt load of money to change my rubber thi…my windshield wipers."

"You got slick in the mouth with him, didn't you?"

"Slick in the what?"

"Let me guess. He called you honey, sweetie, or sugar."

"Missy. He called me, missy, so I corrected him and told him my name is Tess," I said proudly.

"Do you need a valium or something? He's harmless. You're in a small, southern town now. We all have pet names. Good grief, girl. He named me Butterball. That'll probably be put on my gravestone too." She shuffled through the photos. "Dirk is harmless. He'd give you the shirt off his back if you needed it."

I didn't reply but continued to look at the photos. I picked up one of an old woman wearing a tiara. Her banner read, "Worm Grunting Queen."

"Wow. I had no idea a Worm Grunting Queen was something to get excited about."

Butterball rolled her eyes. "I know, I know, it's weird all right. The folks in Sopchoppy live for this. Some actually make a living at worm grunting and a pretty darn good one too."

26

"It sounds like something you would go to the doctor for and stay close to the bathroom with after you started your meds." I chuckled at how funny I was.

"Well, aren't you just a snake in the basket kind of nice." Butterball eyed me carefully. "You drive a wood stake in the ground and rub a piece of iron back and forth across the other end. The vibrations cause the slimy, little critters to bubble up out of the ground. Kernels of popcorn popping...or so I'm told."

The brown spaghetti mystery was solved. "And what is done with these little...non-edible Tootsie Rolls from the earth?"

"Bait. Gotta use something to get that meg," Butterball giggled. "Actually, it is used for bait. There are lots of fishermen around here. It happens every year. This is the fourteenth Sopchoppy Worm Grunting Festival coming up, and I usually get photos for the paper, but I have gall-bladder surgery the day before." Butterball grabbed the photos with shaky hands and slid them back in a folder. "I don't have a backup photographer, so what do you say?"

"Surgery the day before? When is this event?"

"My surgery is scheduled in two weeks, we need to get started on training you for this event." She said this as if I had already signed a contract in blood.

"Next week? I'm just passing through." No way was I staying in this backwoods, hick-infested, one-stoplight town. "I have to be somewhere."

"Oh, yeah, where?" Her inquiring eyes bored into my face, and as I turned away, I could feel them burning a hole in my head.

"Listen, I wasn't born under a hotdog vender, okay? I'm not some crazy lady living with chickens on a beach as some people think. I'm in a bad situation and need help. You can stay here free of rent. I will feed you and your daughter. My niece won't be back for a couple of weeks. You will be long gone by

27

then. You'll have a chance to rest and recoup. I saw the suitcases in the backseat of the thunderbird when you pulled up. It'll give that baby of yours a chance to stretch her legs and walk. And don't worry, I know the perfect person to babysit…years of experience too. Trust me, I have this covered."

Paisley, my algae-eating daughter, bucked at first when I pulled her from the window, ready to get out of there, but she quickly settled down and molded to my hip. The wind picked up more as evidenced by small white caps. An elderly couple was strolling on the beach, holding hands. A gust of wind carried the woman's beach hat up in the air as her husband ran after it and pounced on it in the same manner as a wild animal catching its prey. He returned and placed it gingerly on her head with a tender kiss to her smiling lips. They looked content. I felt it briefly when Paisley and I had our windows down on the washboard road. I might not get a chance like this again with free food and rent.

I turned to Butterball. "What does one wear to a worm grunting festival?"

Butterball screamed and rattled the dishes in the cupboards when she jumped up and down. She hugged me so hard I burped up a little breakfast. Myra Jean's didn't taste as good coming up as it did going down.

CHAPTER FOUR

The rest of the morning was spent listening to Butterball tell me stories of her childhood, her crazy family, and how she got her photography job. She gave me a quick lesson in photography, which was easy to grasp. We took a quick break for a snack and went right back to taking photos in the house.

"See, I told you. You're a natural," she said as she watched me take photos of Paisley. "How old is your daughter?"

"About two years old."

"It will do her good to get out of the car. I take it she isn't walking yet, but she will before you know it."

She sounded confident in Paisley. My mood soured instantly. Time to change the subject.

In no time at all, we were right back to talking about the Worm Grunting Festival as she prepared leftover noodle soup. She brought out ingredients to make homemade biscuits and gently smeared melted butter on the tops before putting them in the oven. My mouth was watering just thinking about them. We set the table with her niece's green and white stoneware, and then I checked out the old CD collection they had. King Cotton Blues was Butterball's choice. Butterball buttered Paisley's biscuit and placed small ham chunks with lima beans on her plate.

"It's perfect finger food for her. This way you can eat, and she can feed herself."

"But she will make a mess," I said.

"Well, we will just clean it up. Didn't your mother or grandmother teach you anything about taking care of babies?"

I forced a smile, pretending I had a fond memory for a moment though I never experienced having a mother, or a grandmother, for that matter. Nope, just me and Dad. Now, just me and Paisley. A huge sigh escaped, before I could stop it, causing Butterball to cast her eyes at me.

"Thank you for the food." I reached for the biscuit and started to shove it in my mouth and saw that Butterball was holding Paisley's hand and looking at me. They both looked at me.

"Yes?"

"We need to say a prayer before we eat."

"Oh." I reached out, clasped hands with Butterball and Paisley, and shut my eyes. Butterball cleared her throat as if preparing for a long speech.

"Bless you, bless me. We won't stand for no blasphemy." She squeezed my hand and released it to get a biscuit. I'd never heard a prayer quite like that before.

"Whatcha waiting for? Eat. He hears all prayers, long and short." She smiled.

Buttery goodness dripped down my forearm when I shoved the biscuit in my mouth. "Oh, Myra Jean's can take a back seat to these," I said as I shoved the rest of the biscuit in my mouth.

"Oh, you better not let the cook at Myra Jean's hear ya," she said as she dipped her biscuit in the steaming chicken broth. "She'll smack the snot right out of you with her spatula." She jerked her hand holding the broth-soaked biscuit in imitation of the cook swinging a spatula. A stream of broth flew across the table and landed on Paisley's forehead. We both burst out laughing when Paisley went cross-eyed trying to see what hit her.

Halfway through the meal, my shoulders relaxed and weren't up to my earlobes. I was slightly enjoying myself for the first time in months in the presence of someone other than

Paisley. I was in a strange town, having supper with a woman named Butterball, planning on staying the night, and I was okay with that. I must have been more exhausted than I thought, or she slipped something in the four biscuits I'd eaten and would be reaching for the ax duct taped under the table. These random thoughts of serial killers that kept popping in my mind had to stop. Again, too much late night television.

As long as she didn't try to corner me into an uncomfortable conversation about Paisley, we would stay a while. And when she did start to pry into my personal life, I would just pry that meg tooth from the limestone, and we'd be on our way.

We cleared the table and washed dishes as Paisley stared out the back window at the ocean.

"If you want to shower before bed, I'll be glad to watch Paisley," she offered.

"I haven't showered alone since we left Alabama. We've always taken them together. Are you serious?"

"Good grief, woman," Butterball said. "I think you need a bubble bath instead. Take a long one too. You'll find lavender-scented soap in the hall closet with the towels. It will help you to relax," she said, and quickly added, "if you believe in miracles."

With towel and lavender soap in hand, I couldn't believe my eyes. Her claw-foot tub was the size of a small car. I would actually be able to submerge my entire body in the tub instead of just my thighs. With the hot water turned on full blast, I placed the chained stopper in the tub. Lavender beads cascaded out of the bottle, melting as they hit the hot steamy water. The aroma filled my nostrils as I peeled out of my clothes and kicked them behind the door. Steam covered the vanity mirror. With one quick swipe, a face appeared. I was barely nineteen but looked forty with dark circles under my eyes. Are those wrinkles? Who gets wrinkles at nineteen? Teenage moms, that's who. Okay, if I was going to relax, I was going all out. I turned

31

on the overhead heater, turned off the lights, and sank into the water. A low rumble from outside echoed in the small bathroom. The ceiling heater roared to life with amber, glowing coils.

The room glowed as red as the old, abandoned plantation home in Alabama that some friends and I stayed in on Halloween night in the ninth grade. My friends and I bought cheap, red solar lights and set them up on the lawn Halloween morning. That night, by the glow of the solar lights, we ate junk food and told horror stories until we were so scared we huddled together. We told each other's parents that we stayed with the other person, otherwise we wouldn't have been there having fun, freezing, and scared to death. By morning, we woke up spooning to keep warm. I miss doing stupid stuff.

Two years of tension began to wash away as I inhaled deeply. White, foamy mountains of bubbles floated across the top of the water and surrounded me. My distorted reflection off the bathtub faucet spout appeared. It was a naked Buddha. Invisible arms pulled me back onto the cushiony bath pillow. I planned on closing my eyes for a minute, just long enough to block out the naked Buddha, but one big sigh later, I was asleep.

CHAPTER FIVE

Inhaling cold water up your nose, when asleep, works better than caffeine. As my eyes fell on the bottle of lavender bath beads, it all came rushing back to me. Oh, my gosh. How long have I been asleep? The house was completely silent. She butchered my Paisley!

A tidal wave of water cascaded over the tub as I jumped out, threw a towel around myself, and bolted for the bathroom door. Once my foot hit the wet linoleum floor, I lost my balance. In a desperate attempt to catch myself, I grabbed for the lavatory and knocked half of Butterball's bath products on the floor to keep myself vertical. Two fingernails snapped in the process. I don't know what hurt more, the spasm in my back as I righted myself or the fingernails that broke at the quick, but I managed to stay upright. That wasn't the case for Butterball's bath products as hundreds of lavender beads rolled across the floor in different directions, ricocheting off other containers as they crashed on the floor. When I bent over to pick up the empty bottle of bath beads, the bathroom door opened.

"What happened?" asked Butterball.

I jerked upright, pulled the towel down over my rear, and somehow managed to keep the girls covered up. I swear the manufacturers were making smaller bath towels, because this one was barely keeping my butt cheeks covered.

"You haven't broken anything, have you?" she asked, examining the contents on the floor.

"No, no. I didn't. I'm fine. Thanks for asking."

Two little boys peeked around the doorframe and gawked at me, half wrapped in a towel. I could not have been more embarrassed. Two hands reached out and yanked the boys back by their shirt collars out of view of the bathroom.

"Where is Paisley?" I demanded.

"She's asleep in the spare bedroom, but maybe not after all this racket."

"She'll roll off the bed. You can't leave her alone," I fussed, while trying to get out of the bathroom. Butterball placed her arm across the threshold, blocking my exit.

"Dirk brought a crib down from his house. I thought you might enjoy getting a night's rest in the bed by yourself. She is perfectly fine, but you might want to put clothes on before you come out...unless you want to meet the Ramsey family *au natural*." She walked away, but flipped around. "F-Y-I, I do know a few things about babies. It's a side effect from the two I had."

I grabbed my dirty clothes and slipped out of the bathroom and into the bedroom. Paisley was asleep on her stomach. Her body stretched out in imitation of a person strapped to a gurney. Usually, she curled up in a ball, but she looked as relaxed as I'd been in the tub. Butterball had apparently taken my luggage out of the car while I was in the tub and placed it on the bed.

A drop of water fell from the tip of my damp hair and plopped on Paisley's cheek. It didn't faze her. I dressed in clean clothes and towel-dried my hair. Maybe I could stall and the Ramsey's would leave. I really didn't want to see Dirk again, not after the windshield wiper incident. The offer of money is what pulled me here, nothing else. New friends are not something I was interested in. They all left me anyway. Plus, I had no plans to stay here long enough for friends to do me any good. I went to the bathroom in search of a blow dryer and caught sight of myself in the mirror. The dark circles were less noticeable. I dried my hair for so long, procrastinating the visit with Dirk, that I created new split ends.

They stood on the back porch, watching clouds roll in. Dark clouds—not the soft, gray ones that filled the sky earlier—stretched above us. It was time to face the inevitable. The warmth of the house left my skin when I opened the French doors. Cold, salty air hit me.

Dirk turned, smiled, and winked. His wife smacked him in the arm and gave me a pitiful look, showing she was embarrassed for me. Her long, ebony hair matched her coal-colored eyes. Black eyes usually gave me the chills, but hers were comforting and full of tenderness. They were the eyes of a mother.

"This is going to be a big storm," he said. "We'll probably get rain all night and through tomorrow morning." He rubbed his arms briskly. "I can feel the cold front coming in too. March weather is always odd. Florida is the only place I know that has freaky weather like this. Hot one minute and cold the next."

"Aren't you working on Lenny's truck tomorrow?" his wife asked.

"Yeah, but I'll be done by ten a.m., plenty of time to take the boys fishing." His boys jumped around in excitement. "Butterball, you can keep the crib as long as you need it. No rush getting it back to us."

They visited for another two hours, talking about nothing important, while I preoccupied myself with the two boys putting a puzzle together. A loud rumble of thunder made Dirk's eyebrows raise.

"We need to get home before this storm lets loose," Said Dirk as he patted his wife on the leg. They said their good-byes and headed down the street before the downpour.

"How far do they live from here?"

"Just about half a mile," Butterball answered.

"They walked half a mile dragging a crib down this bumpy road?" I asked in astonishment.

"That's Dirk for ya. When he was a child, he had polio, and the doctors told him he would never walk again. He proved them wrong. He walks every chance he gets, if it's not too far."

Butterball closed the French doors as the wind picked up, chilling the air. She headed for the fireplace. "I'll get the fire going tonight in case we lose power. Sometimes with wind as strong as this, it messes with the power lines. We don't usually set a fire this early, but this house is an old one and not insulated well. Cold outside means cold inside. You can come out here if it does, but I think the blankets will keep you warm enough. I already fed Paisley. She should be good for a few hours. There are fixings for a sandwich in the refrigerator, and chips are above the microwave. I'm heading to bed. Good night."

Butterball slipped into the master bedroom and moved about. The toilet flushed, she gargled, and the light from under the door was extinguished. Within ten minutes, food stretched from one end of her counter to the other. My plate was full of purple grapes, pimento cheese sandwiches, potato salad, and ham from earlier. I polished it off with coffee ice cream and purred as contented as a kitten. There was no one there to stop me, and I was in heaven with all this food.

The house was quiet except for the crackle of the fire and the angry thunder outside. Flashes of lightning streaked across the sky, lighting up the living room for a fraction of a second. Paisley slept right through it.

The last home I was in was with Dad. I thought of going to the bedroom to sleep. I'd almost forgotten the feel of a good mattress under my body, but we won't be here long, so why get used to it. I stayed on the couch in front of the fire. The pink and white pinwheel quilt, draped over the back of the couch, swallowed me as I nestled down. Flickers of red, blue, orange, and purple rolled over the logs. Fluorescent-orange, jagged lines crisscrossed over the embers and pulsed with the heat. The sky fell open on Butterball's tin roof. It was either those dang biscuits again, or she sprinkled powdered valium over those logs, because I was out, *again*, before I knew it.

***

I was dreaming—or at least I hoped I was. I was back in the hospital, and Paisley had just been born. This time I wasn't alone. Several people in white uniforms surrounded the clear, plastic baby bed she was in. They separated her from the other children in the nursery and placed her bed across the room.

"Why is she so far away from the others?" I asked.

A faceless nurse turned to me. "Get used to it, doll. She'll be separated from them for the rest of her life." And with that comment, she turned and walked away. My wrists were restrained with soft cuffs making it impossible to get to Paisley. I yelled for help when I noticed my ankles were strapped down too. Several nurses arrived and tried to muffle my screams with their hands. A male technician pulled out a needle and thumped it to get the air out.

"No, don't!" I struggled to get free, but the restraints stopped me, and he jabbed it in my arm.

"That should quiet her down. Now, to get rid of that baby. It doesn't belong here." He walked to Paisley's bassinet where she was swaddled in blankets and picked her up. He looked at me for a moment, smirked, and tossed the blankets in the air.

When they floated back down, there was no baby. He smiled at his carnival trick, as I tried to scream, but the medicine had taken affect and dulled my senses. Their faces blurred, and voices garbled together as if speaking under water. I screamed, but didn't hear my voice. "Can't anyone hear me? Get my baby!"

"You didn't want her, remember? Your life wasn't supposed to turn out this way," the technician taunted me. "Go build that white picket fence, little girl."

"But I want my daughter," I tried to mumble.

37

"That's not what we heard you thinking," he teased.

I tried to reach a compromise with them. "Can't you just take the Down syndrome away and leave my daughter?"

"Nope. It's a package deal. No exchanges. It's all or nothing. You get what you get, and don't cry a bit." He lit a cigarette and a nurse reprimanded him for doing it around the other babies. She tried to take it from him, but he held it high out of her reach, not realizing he was holding the burning cigarette a mere two inches from the overhead sprinkler. The fire alarm went off, and I bolted awake.

"Good morning," said Butterball as she moved the whistling teapot from the front burner to the back one. My fire alarm silenced. "Sorry I woke you. Did you sleep on the couch all night?"

Yesterday's clothes were wrinkled and plastered to my body from sweat. The fire was completely cold. My heart still raced from the nightmare. "I guess so," I said and cast the pink pinwheel quilt to the side.

"Paisley has already eaten her breakfast. She loves pancakes." Small, sticky fingers touched my hand. Paisley held on to me for balance. She's still here. I grabbed her and squeezed her tightly to my chest for reassurance. As she laid her cheek on my shoulder, facing me, I smelled the sweet maple syrup on her breath.

"Come eat before it gets cold. There's sausage too." Butterball dished out our food, and I watched as she slowly poured the steaming water into mugs filled with instant cocoa. "Let's move to the porch. Sometimes I get a show in the mornings."

"What kind of show?"

"Dolphins. They come in close to get fish near the shore."

Paisley reared back, wanting me to put her down. She crawled with one foot and one knee to get to Butterball. We carried our mountain of pancakes to the porch and fell into the lawn chairs. Everything on the back porch was covered in dew.

"This will clear up in no time, honey. Once the sun comes out, it will be as dry as my love life. We had quite a storm last night. It took out power a few streets over. Glad it didn't reach us. Glad the freakish Florida cold front blew over too." She silenced herself with sausage in her mouth.

Butterball's sausage-filled cheeks were puffed out like a blowfish. Paisley scooted to the railing, letting her chubby legs dangle through the slats, swinging them back and forth as she stared at the water.

The entire sky was still gray from last night's storm. The beach was deserted. A few small birds scurried across the shoreline, pecking at seaweed thrown ashore during the storm. There was no traffic, no people. Just nothing. Last night's nightmare faded fast. Remnants of the cold front whipped around in the air with warm spots from the sun straining to break through the few peepholes in the clouds. When it did, it felt warm on my face.

"Your pancakes are gonna get cold," Butterball said with a mouthful of breakfast. "Ain't nothing worse than cold pancakes." I reached for my plate, but the sausage was gone. Butterball's guilty look of pleasure clued me in to the fate of my sausage. "Well, it was getting cold too. There's more inside if you want some." She paused. "What say we go into town? I can show you around," Butterball suggested. "You can practice with my camera."

"Sounds good. What is there to see in this town?" I teased.

"A few stop signs," she said and laughed. "No, really, Wakulla ain't that bad. You just have to know where to look. Wakulla Springs is a start. We can get shots of alligators on the banks and white ibis."

"What is a white ibis?"

"They're all over the place down here. Anywhere you see standing water, you'll eventually see one. They are covered in white feathers, except the tips of their wings are black, and their pink beaks are almost as long as their bodies. Sorta odd looking."

"Ah, I have seen one. It made me think of a stork."

"Oh, and they are monogamous too. Just thought I'd throw a bit of trivia in there." Butterball giggled at her comment. An awkward silence followed, and she must have felt a need to explain, so she continued. "You never know when the information might come in handy. You might be a contestant on Jeopardy," she said. "You'll thank me one day."

I had to get us back on track. "What is there to do at Wakulla Springs?"

Butterball took the bait and smiled. "You have shorts, right?" Without giving me time to answer, she continued. "They have a jungle boat ride, which Paisley would love. They have a glass-bottom boat ride and a two-tier tower that you can jump off of, but you better enjoy it while you can. It used to be a three-tier but they tore the top one down for safety reasons. Oh, my gosh, we have to go canoeing. Have you ever been? You get the best shots because you can get down in these areas…"

I listened to her rattle on for a few more minutes without my input. Finally, I decided to just tell her I would go so she would stop talking.

"Look, look," Butterball pointed toward the water. There was nothing at first. Then, a small, curved fin broke the water's surface and disappeared just as quickly. Not one, but two, dolphins broke the surface again and went back under. They jumped periodically, playing with each other. We sat mesmerized by their activity. I'd never seen one before.

"Have you ever gotten closer?" I asked.

"Oh, yes. I was wading out here one time when I was a little girl. One came close to me. At first, all I saw was a fin above the surface and I thought it was a shark. I remembered that a shark's fin has sharp angles, whereas a dolphin's tilts back and has a gentle curve. It came almost close enough for me to touch it." She smiled at the memory.

"Maybe we will have time to go wading one afternoon," Butterball said.

Maybe, I thought.

A few minutes later, I was dressed in khaki shorts and a gray tank top over my borrowed bathing suit, which belonged to Butterball's niece. Paisley wore a yellow sundress with sandals. She snuggled close on my hip.

Butterball continuously slammed and opened her closet door and chest of drawers. A loud crash was followed by her yelling, "I'm okay." In a sudden rush, she emerged from the bedroom with arms full and her legs spread out to balance herself. All I could see were her chunky, ivory-colored legs, her bright green shorts, and her hands. She was loaded down with two cameras, two camera cases, five huge beach towels, and other odds and ends piled high on the beach towels. Her wide-brimmed beach hat on top of her head spanned the width of her shoulders. It bobbled about, above the towels, as she moved. "I think I forgot something."

"Do you want help?" I offered.

"No, dear. I want my knuckles to drag on the ground caveman style. Of course I do. Now get your ass over here."

I grabbed the wicker basket, which was full of food, off the kitchen counter, and hung the cameras with their cases around my neck. Paisley played with the zipper on one of the cases. We piled into her SUV and, as she turned the keys, her radio blasted the Beach Boys at top volume. She giggled in embarrassment. "I'm usually alone in the car." She quickly turned it down. "I thought about auditioning for one of those talent shows on television, but Dirk eloquently suggested I not."

"What did he say?"

"He said I sounded like an animal being neutered without anesthesia."

"I think I'm starting to appreciate Dirk." I tried to suppress a giggle, but a snort came out instead. She glared at me.

41

"I just need to warm up, that's all," she said. "I sing wonderfully in the shower."

"Don't we all?"

CHAPTER SIX

Half way to Wakulla Springs, Butterball gave up singing when Paisley started to cry.

"What brings you to Wakulla County?" Butterball inquired.

Here we go, the start of a disaster. "Just taking a little vacation," I mumbled. She looked at me, and I knew she didn't buy my answer, but she didn't ask any more questions and started to hum. I pressed my cheek against the cool glass and watched the gray asphalt whiz by in a blur.

This was the longest I'd been around the same person since we left Alabama. I was used to just being around Paisley, and let's face it, she wasn't much of a conversationalist. I wasn't sure if I remembered how to carry on a conversation in which I received actual feedback that wasn't in the form of a mumble or a cry. Pretty soon, she was going to start asking personal questions again—where I was from, did I have any family—all those things that were none of her business. How was I supposed to handle this? Should I have recited name, rank, and serial number? I wouldn't be here long enough to worry about being friends. I didn't need a friend. What I needed was her money, and Paisley and I would be gone. She was considered my bed and breakfast for the next couple of weeks. I'd just have to make the best of it.

Butterball went back to singing instead of humming. She looked in the rearview mirror at Paisley and smiled. I heard Paisley over my shoulder, making noises, long drawn-out noises. I think she was trying to sing, but the sound that came from her mouth…. Let's just say a wounded moose that I saw on the National Geographic channel once carried a tune better than her. Eventually, I began tapping my foot to the beat of the song.

If I'd been driving, I might have missed the park or been slammed from behind. The woods were thick right up to the entrance. Butterball turned in, pulled up to a building resembling a toll booth, and paid our fare to the attendant.

"You taking more pictures, Butterball?" asked the attendant.

"Of course. Are the glass-bottom boats running today?"

"Yes."

"Glass-bottom? Isn't that dangerous?" I asked with concern.

They laughed at me. "She's not from around here," Butterball offered as explanation, and the attendant nodded.

Once we passed the small building, we moved at a turtle's pace down the winding road. Low-lying spots with standing water dotted the road on either side. Small cypress trees grew, stretching toward the sun in competition with the taller trees. Squirrels played tag with the wheels of Butterball's car as they scampered across the road, jumping to the nearest hickory or beech tree in victory.

Before my eyes, a castle appeared. At least to me it looked akin to one. The two-story building was built in a Mediterranean style with a red slate roof that covered creamy-beige, exterior walls. Every window was arched and stretched as tall as some of the trees in the park.

"Let's go in the lodge first before we unload, but bring the camera so you can get photos," she encouraged.

With Paisley on my hip and Butterball carrying the camera equipment, we followed the hexagonal, earthy-colored pavers to the entrance which was covered with a red-domed canopy. The marble floor was slick under my flip flops, compared to the

44

concrete. Though the shine was worn off the marble floor due to age, it was still a sight to see. The ceilings, at least thirty feet high, had crisscrossing, wooden beams. The artwork on the ceiling was detailed and fine. I would have sworn it was just painted the day before. I should have paid more attention in art history, because I would have known what period the décor and paint were from. It was beautiful. Arched windows, spanning almost to the ceiling, were on the far wall of the lobby, facing the springs. Each one was at least twelve feet wide. To the left, just after the check-in desk, was an enormous limestone fireplace. This thing was large enough to stand in. There was a baby grand in the lobby just outside the dining area. Through the partially shut doors to the dining room, I could hear the clink of utensils and the low mumble of dinner conversation. Everywhere I looked, there was something else to take in.

"Hey, when was this place built?"

"In the late 1930s. You'll see art deco designs all over the place."

I was still staring at the ceiling when Butterball dragged me across the lobby. "I want you to meet someone." I bumped into something hard and turned around to see alligator teeth a mere foot from my thighs. There, before me, was a huge alligator with its mouth gaped open, glossy black in coloring, encased in a glass, coffin-like structure.

"Some idiot shot him in the late sixties. He was known as Ole Joe to the locals. The owners of the springs thought it would be educational to stuff him and show him off to tourists. Personally, I would rather have a great pair of cowboy boots, and maybe a clutch, for church on Sundays."

I was dumbstruck by her comments and simply stared.

"What?" she asked. "I have been known to attend once in a while. It's not too far out of the ordinary."

"I'm going to see a lot of alligators out here?"

"More than just alligators. I guess at your age, this is pretty boring, but you need to practice somewhere, and I want a little sun."

We exited the back entrance and took the gently sloped pavers down toward the springs. Butterball quickly found a partially shady spot under a tall, skinny cypress tree, and I spread out the towels. Little girls ran around with floaties on their arms, and wet, sagging bathing suits flapped on their butts. A Speedo barely covered an old man's rear as he dipped his toes in the water. He instantly retracted them and his face drew up in the fashion of someone sucking on sour pickles. He retreated to his wife's side on a beach towel to read a book.

A group of teenagers walked down the pier and up the stairs of the two-tier tower. Several girls formed a circle in the center of the tower to avoid being bumped into the frigid water below. In a rush, one guy broke through the crowd of girls and yelled "Geronimo" as he flung his skinny body over the edge. His high-pitched, shrilly, girl scream filled the air as he rocketed over the side of the tower into the water below. The girls he was trying to impress leaned over to watch as his body pierced the water like a knife. A few seconds later, he surfaced, minus his shorts. Laughter of boys and girls filled the air as he swam to retrieve them. It was obvious that they had fun up there, hanging out with friends, laughing at themselves, and at each other.

I missed that. I watched a few minutes more as they continued to drop off the top tier into the water below while others swam to a nearby floating dock.

"That tickles, Mommy," said a sweet child's voice from behind me. When I reached to straighten out my towel, I saw a woman tickling her daughter, and I couldn't help smiling.

"How old is she?" I asked.

"She just turned twenty-five months," she beamed. "How old is your daughter?"

"About the same age," I answered and watched as the toddler walked to her mom's tote bag and brought her the suntan lotion while trying to open it. When the mom squirted the lotion in the palms of her hands, the daughter automatically turned to get lotioned up.

Paisley should have been doing all these same things. But no, my Paisley discovered a small stick that I had apparently kicked up on the blanket. She stared at it while little Miss Einsteinetta flourished behind us. In frustration, I yanked it out of her hand and threw it in the water. Why should I believe that today would be any different than any other day? I should have known there would be children here her age.

My eyes closed as I flopped back on the towel. Within ten seconds, Butterball was laughing. Annoyed, I cracked one eye open. A black Labrador had retrieved the stick I had thrown and plopped it in Paisley's lap. In her excitement at seeing a dog, she grabbed its fur and pulled herself to a standing position. This was a first for Paisley, to pull herself up to a standing position, but it didn't last long enough to enjoy. The dog shook violently, ridding itself of the excess water, and drenched all three of us in the process. Paisley let go immediately and fell on her bottom.

"Get out of here," I yelled with flailing arms. The dog retreated, but Butterball was still laughing.

"Newsflash, you are at Wakulla Springs. You are going to get wet." Butterball giggled at her comment.

I was fuming. "Just leave me alone."

"Seriously, Tess, you need to relax. Do you really want to be alone?"

"Yes, from everyone."

"You okay with me taking Paisley on the boat ride? You can just do whatever it is you need to do."

The thought of someone taking Paisley away from me made me want to say no, but it was just a boat cruise. It wasn't as if she was kidnapping my baby. They had to come back. I'd just watch them leave…to be sure.

"Thank you," I said and watched as the jungle boat loaded up with spectators. And it hit me. I was alone at a beach, well sort of a beach. I could close my eyes and soak up the sun without watching Paisley—and be a carefree teenager again. It was me time, finally. Ah, sun on my skin. I hadn't felt this in a long time.

Yep, I was alone, without Paisley and her chubby arms reaching for me. No silly giggling or sighs as she fell asleep. No sticky, syrupy fingers touching me. Why did my chest feel heavy? I didn't realize I had been clinching my jaw until it started to hurt. I tried to shake off this feeling of depression, but it lingered.

"Breathe, Tess. Just relax," I whispered to myself. "This is what you've been wanting for a while now." Maybe the pain in my chest was just heartburn. Sitting up didn't diminish it. I pulled out Butterball's camera and fiddled with it for a minute, reminding myself of the settings that Butterball showed me, and I went into full paparazzi mode. Nothing escaped the camera. Not the water, eelgrass, trees, kids jumping off the tiers, not even the small water snake gliding through the water, causing children to do their best interpretation of Jesus walking on water. When a teenage boy caught it and threw it in the woods by the tower, people started to venture back in.

The floating dock was packed with kids. One very pale, blond-haired kid had an inner tube around him as he tried to get the courage to go back in the water. He must have been on the dock for a while, because his hair was dry. Two younger children wrestled over a toy next to him and the bigger of the two shoved the smaller one into the inner-tube kid. He immediately bounced off the inner tube into the water. It reminded me of a pinball machine, and I caught it all on film.

I headed toward the area where the jungle boat departed. An Asian man with a meticulously groomed white beard that came to a point at the tip sat on a park bench. He sported an orange bandana over his head. While everyone else was in swim attire, he sat there in jeans and a long-sleeved shirt. He was so out of his element, I had to get a photo of him.

"Excuse me, sir, do you mind if I take a photo of you?"

I took his nod as a yes and proceeded to snap photos when he suddenly jumped. "What are you doing?"

He caught me off guard. "You said I could take photos of you."

"You heard me say that?" he asked and looked angry.

"Well, not exactly. You nodded your head."

"I was falling asleep. Didn't you see my eyes closed? Stupid tourist," he said just above a whisper for me to hear.

"Sorry," I mumbled and quickly walked back to the towels. Miss Einsteinetta played with her shovel and pail while Mom leaned back in her beach chair, reading a gossip magazine. Both of them looked as content as could be. If I must be saddled with a baby, why couldn't it have been one like Einsteinetta? She handled and maneuvered the shovel in ways I might never see Paisley do. There was that heartburn again. I left the happy duo and headed back down the dock just as the jungle boat pulled up.

Paisley stood on the seat, looking over the edge at the churning, clear water. Butterball had a firm grasp on her waist. As they unloaded the crew from the boat, she carried Paisley on her hip. Paisley was excited from the boat ride, and she bucked and kicked Butterball vigorously. You would have thought Butterball was a Kentucky Derby race horse and Paisley was the jockey. Butterball grinned from ear to ear.

"We had a great time, didn't we, Paisley?"

Paisley bucked more, and I noticed sweat beading on Butterball's upper lip.

"I'll take her."

"That's okay. I got her." She resisted, and Paisley withdrew into Butterball's ample breasts. "Did you get pictures?"

"A few."

"I'm starving. I think I packed fried chicken," Butterball said as we headed for the towels.

Butterball ripped the foil off the drumstick and sank her teeth in. She looked at me with grease surrounding her lips, reminding me of a child discovering lip gloss for the first time. "This reminds me, I need to check on the chickens when we get home."

The insulated lunch bag held more chicken, potato salad, grapes, three small ice cream sandwiches, tooth paste, and a tooth brush. I reached for an ice cream sandwich. Pretty soon I'd be known as Butterball Junior if I kept eating. I found napkins and sporks tucked in a side pocket, but nothing to dish the potato salad out in. She must have read my mind.

"Just share it with Paisley. I'm good."

She didn't have to tell me twice. I dug in and gave Paisley a few bites, expecting her not to like it. She spit out everything else I gave her, why not this too? Her eyes lit up at the taste of something new. It bothered me that she knew my Paisley better than me. Her likes and dislikes. I'd been with her since birth. Butterball had spent one day with her and already knew more about my own daughter than I did. Paisley smacked her hand on the potato salad container, causing mayo to fly up in her hair. She polished off her lunch with grape halves.

"Someone is watching you," Butterball said.

"What?"

"The young man over by the dock. The guys always check out the newbies." Butterball nudged my arm, prompting me to look up.

"Well, this newbie ain't interested."

"Too late. Here he comes."

It was the snake guy. He must have been at least six feet two inches tall and in his early twenties. What shocked me the most was that his smile kept getting bigger the closer he came. His confidence made me think of Thom and how he had

50

approached me. That bothered me. Maybe if I picked my nose, he would go away.

"Hey."

"Hey," I repeated back.

Butterball dug around in the lunch container and pretended to look for something. The lunch container was only so big. Whatever she was looking for, she would have found by now. She definitely was not good at pretending to be occupied.

"You from here?" he tried again.

"Nope," I answered.

"Where are you from?"

"Not here," I said with a sigh and looked out at the water. Maybe he would get the hint. Walk away, little man. Walk away.

Obviously, he was still interested. "Cute sister."

"She's not my sister. She's my daughter," I said with finality, knowing this would be the nail in the coffin of this meet and greet session.

He didn't flinch at my comment. "Can you swim?"

Can you take a hint? "Do you think I would be near water if I couldn't?" Geez, this guy was as dense as breast tissue.

Butterball cut her eyes over at me and took Paisley in her arms.

"My little sister has arm floaties if you need them. I just figured you've never been around large bodies of water with your pale color," he said with a smirk.

Butterball snorted and quickly looked away. This guy was really pissing me off. I was seconds away from telling him off when he said I'd have to prove it by jumping off the top tier— just like in elementary school on the playground at recess when Bobbie Jo Whitehouse double-dog-dared me to walk barefoot on the top of the monkey bars.

"You can't stop, not even once if you want my Ho Hos," she teased. I wanted those Ho Hos *bad*. I had blisters on the soles of my feet for a week from the hot, metal bars, but I got those Ho Hos.

"If I do this, will you go away and leave me alone?"

"Deal," he said with a smile, and we sealed it with a sweaty handshake.

"Butterball, do you mind watching Paisley?" I asked as I stood up, ready to take on this challenge.

"Not at all." She beckoned me to lean forward. As I did, she grabbed my shirt at the collar and pulled me face-to-face. "You do know how to swim, right?"

"Better than a mermaid," I said to reassure her. I might not have been near a beach growing up, but my best friend Gabrielle had a pool in her backyard. We swam all the time, until she moved away during our senior year.

I peeled out of my clothes and adjusted the loaner, one-piece bathing suit while I walked toward the tower. As I got closer, it quadrupled in size. It reminded me of those "sea monkeys" my dad said he used to send off for in a magazine. "Just add water and watch them grow," it advertised.

Once I reached the foot of the Eiffel Tower, I took a deep breath. He was already up the ladder before I knew it. He looked down, smiling in anticipation of me calling it off. I decided he wasn't going to get the satisfaction. As I climbed up the ladder, the sun beat down on me. Fifteen or so other people laughed as they enjoyed being on a platform, forty feet in the air, and without a railing.

I held my hand up, visor-like, to block the sun as I looked over the treetops across the bank. Was the air thinner up here, or was it just me? People scattered all about in the colorless water. Some floated. Others swam. Butterball played patty cake with Paisley on the bank to my right. The jungle cruise took on more passengers for another tour and headed down the river. I'd never seen water so clear. The bottom appeared to be a few feet deep, but I knew better. Just when I started to get the nerve to jump, I saw something blackish, green, and scaly across the

52

bank from the tower. Old Joe's great-great-great-grandson was basking on the bank, eyeballing everyone, trying to decide who he wanted for lunch. How fast could an alligator swim? Tarzan always made it out okay, in the old movies. But, then again, I wasn't Jane. No one else noticed him. He turned and disappeared into the woods. I tried to figure out how to get out of this when the guy walked up and stood beside me.

"How deep is this?" I asked to prepare myself.

"Twenty-two feet," he said.

That's not too bad, I thought.

"That's at the ledge. It drops to over one hundred feet once you get off the ledge," he added.

The YMCA never talked to us about alligators. I'd never be found. Gators would get my body and stuff it in a beaver house. Paisley would be raised by chickens and a woman named Butterball. I turned to tell him he won the bet when a skinny girl with bulging eyes bumped me and knocked me clean off the tower. On the way down, I saw on the far bank, amongst the tall grass, the gator was back, and his eyes were focused on me.

"Gator!" I shrieked.

My body hit the water, and I knew what the *Titanic* survivors felt. A million needles pierced all over my body. I took back what I said about not being found. I'd be found, all right—in an iceberg floating down the Wakulla River. My body started to feel numb, and I couldn't distinguish which way was up. Bubbles surrounded me, and the pressure in my chest was crushing me from holding my breath. Two hands grabbed my forearms and yanked me to the surface. Sputtering and dazed, my face was a mere two inches from the idiot who talked me into this. He must have jumped just seconds after I did.

He smiled at me. "Woo-hoo! Makes you feel alive, don't it?" He shook the water from his hair, and it pierced my eyeballs.

"I ffffeel like a pppopsssicle."

"Your lips do look a little blue. But it's a pretty blue. Actually, more like teal."

I was so cold, I could barely tread water. He led me to the ladder on the side of the dock where two girls hauled my butt up. I stood shivering, arms straight down with elbows locked, and teeth chattering loud enough to chip my enamel.

"Chance," he said.

"No. Not a chance in hell am I going to do that again," I sputtered.

He laughed. "No, my *name* is Chance."

"Well, Chance, I am going to throw my body on the hood of a car to warm up. See ya," I said, and I stormed off.

"If it's worth anything, I give you a nine point five on the jump," he hollered as I walked away.

I turned around to say something obnoxious, but he'd already moved on to his next unsuspecting prey, which happened to be a cute, little, teenage girl who was sunning on the bank and perfectly dry. She wouldn't be for long.

Butterball handed me a towel as I collapsed.

"I had no idea the water was this cold."

"He didn't tell you?" she asked.

"Nope," I answered. I briskly towel-dried my hair, and the towel fell to my waist. I tilted my face to the sun and prayed for a solar flare to shoot out a few hundred miles so I would feel warm again.

"Um, you might want to keep covered up a little bit longer," Butterball said.

"Why?"

"Your chest resembles a Braille book."

I took her word for it and readjusted my towel. The adrenaline rush of jumping off the tower reminded me of all the other stupid stunts I'd done: riding my bike downhill with my eyes closed, racing across my neighbor's yard when I wasn't sure if their German shepherd, Hercules, was on the chain or not, having unprotected sex with Thom. That was when I had no

54

responsibilities whatsoever. When I was pushed off the tower and hit the frigid water, I was instantly brought back to reality. That was exactly the kind of stunt I would have done pre-Paisley. I couldn't believe I'd just done that.

Couldn't I just go back in time? Not much, just two and a half years. Two and a half years was such a small amount of time, really. I wanted a chance to be a kid again and to go out with friends, flirt with guys on the college campus, and honk the horn as they practiced football on the fields. But I'd make sure I didn't get involved with them—any of them. I'd learned my lesson. I promise. I'd focus more on school, maybe go to college. I would have choices that had been taken away from me. One day when I was ready, I wanted to fall in love and have someone love me back. And when I got pregnant, I wanted him never to doubt that the baby was his. Most of all, I wanted him to stay with me and not run off to play soccer in college. Was that too much to ask? Just a little happiness in my life would be nice.

"Did you put sunscreen on?" Butterball asked, interrupting my thoughts.

"No."

"You should." I felt a cold bottle lay against my neck. Could she possibly be any more irritating than she was? I reached over without looking, squirted the contents out in my palm, and quickly smeared it on my face and shoulders, hoping it would satisfy her. Butterball's high-pitched laughter filled the air. She pointed at my face without comment while her whole body jiggled with laughter. Paisley picked up a tube of toothpaste from where my head was and dropped it in the beach bag. Oh, no, I didn't. The smell of wintergreen filled my nostrils.

This was unbelievable. Toothpaste was smeared on my face and shoulders. I grabbed my T-shirt and wiped my face so hard that I felt the abrasions in the toothpaste exfoliate my skin.

"Toothpaste?" I screamed. "Who brings toothpaste to the beach?"

Butterball stood up defensively, her hands perched on her padded hips. "You shouldn't neglect your teeth. We had fried chicken. Do you want to walk around with dead poultry stuck between your teeth?" She sat back down in a huff. "And we aren't at a beach," she corrected. "We are at The Springs."

"Why are you letting her play with toothpaste anyway?"

"Well, maybe if you brought toys for your daughter, she wouldn't have gotten into it. I had no idea I would get dinner and a show when we came here."

I hated her right then, and the remains of the toothpaste had started to dry on my skin, tightening it. "Where is the bathroom?"

She pointed silently behind her and talked to Paisley as if I wasn't there. I stormed in the direction of the bathroom. Toothpaste. She was just crazy. I'd never seen anyone brush their teeth at the beach, springs, or wherever we were. Two preteen girls rushed ahead of me on the way to the bathroom.

I wanted my dad back. I wanted Dad before the cancer shared rent with his body, before it made him too weak to walk or talk. Before he lost fifty pounds and his skin became cling wrap on his bones. My old, yellow-painted room with its junky chandelier was my safe place. I insisted my dad buy that chandelier for me at a yard sale when I was eight, because I thought princesses had them in their rooms. We spent three days in the dark as he figured out how to wire it. I wanted all my teddy bears back that he gave me each Christmas, even the ones with missing eyes and mangy fur. I wanted them back just because *he* gave them to me. I should never have thrown them out on my sixteenth birthday, trying to prove to him I was a grown up. I wanted to hear the alarm of the old Big Ben clock Dad put by my bed so I wouldn't be late for school. All the annoying things from my childhood—I wanted them back.

But I didn't want the annoying things I had now, such as Paisley. I seriously must have been missing maternal genes or something. Maybe I was never meant to be a mother. Some people just aren't programmed for it. I'd seen specials on television where the mother took her twelve children to the Himalayan Mountains and tossed them off, one by one. I must have Post-Paisley Depression.

The girls giggled in the stalls next to me for no reason in particular, probably just happy to be young. I remembered looking at my friends when we were that age and bursting out in spontaneous laughter. We didn't know why. We just did. They smiled at me, washed their hands, had a ten-second water fight, and raced out. Paisley would never have those kinds of relationships.

"Pull yourself together." I splashed cold water on my face one more time. A flyer was taped to the tile on the bathroom wall. "Adoption is Love – Give the gift of life to another family." Vertical strips on perforated paper, with the business telephone number listed, hung below the bold-typed words. Three pieces were already ripped off. I made it four and stepped out.

CHAPTER SEVEN

When I returned, Butterball was waiting with everything packed. Just another afternoon ruined. The ride home was quiet. Paisley dozed in her car seat. Butterball tuned in to a news station to kill the silence. I assumed my previous position with my forehead glued to the window and watched the trees go by as if they had somewhere to be. Trapped, that's what I was, trapped, and I didn't know why when nothing was physically keeping me here. There was no obligation to her as I hadn't signed any paperwork to do the photography. She wasn't family, just a strange woman I'd met and decided to help out. I could have packed up and been gone by morning. It wasn't my responsibility to help her. Maybe Dirk down the street, or his wife, could help her out. Okay, decision made. I'd be out of here that night, but I thought we'd at least stay for supper so our stomachs would be full.

Not much was said the rest of the afternoon. I fiddled with the camera settings and hoped she wouldn't come over if she thought I was studying. I was wrong. She asked me to feed the chickens for her.

"Feed the chickens?"

"It's pretty simple. Just make sure they have fresh feed and water. They might have kicked around the hay in their coop. If they did, just use the hoe and shove it back in. No need to clean it. I'll do that later." When she noticed I hadn't moved yet, she physically turned me in the direction of the kitchen. "Get a few cherry tomatoes from the refrigerator. They're gentle, even Paisley could hand-feed them."

With Paisley on my hip and a handful of bright red cherry tomatoes, I ventured into the unknown chicken arena. The chickens clucked louder as we approached and paced back and forth. I'd never seen a chicken in person before, at least not a live one. They resembled mini-feathered bowling balls with beaks. I wasn't scared of bowling balls. I'd just focus on that. *Feathered bowling balls, feathered bowling balls.*

"Hey Paisley, do you want them fried or grilled?" I put Paisley down and handed her a tomato to distract the chickens as I opened the coop and tossed the tomatoes a few feet into the pen. The chickens pranced around to get their treats. The food looked good, but the water tower was slightly tilted. I walked into the coop to straighten it out. One of the chickens saw the tomato Paisley was holding. At first, all was good as the chicken gingerly walked toward her, but when it snatched the tomato from her hand, Paisley hit a high note that almost made my eyeballs ooze out of their sockets.

It all happened fast after that. The tomato fell on the ground in the coop. The other chickens saw the luscious red ball and galloped—if a chicken can gallop—toward the coop. I was cornered inside, feeling like the last pin standing at a bowling alley as the feathered bowling balls ran toward me. In a panic, I lost my footing and fell on the tomato. Wings flapped so hard that feathers flew off their bodies, and chicken feet ran across my body in an attempt to get remnants of the tomato I had smashed on my shirt. They pecked at my breast and stomach, and Paisley had the best seat in the house as she held onto the outside of the coop and watched. I felt a scream build up inside me, and I let it loose. Suddenly, I was dragged by my ankles from the coop as Butterball closed the door. I lay there in sand, hay, feathers, and chicken poop while looking up at an angry Butterball.

"You're gonna scare those chickens so bad they won't lay eggs for weeks. What on Earth are you doing?"

"What am I doing? Those feathered freaks attacked me," I shrieked.

"Let's see, you're afraid of heights, water, and chickens. Is there anything else I should know?"

I'm afraid of spending the rest of my life alone or alone with Paisley. "Nope, that about sums it up," I said as I went back inside. I went into the bathroom and screamed, making my throat spasm. When I emerged they were both in the living room.

"Do you feel better?"

"No."

Butterball occupied Paisley with some pots and pans to play with in the kitchen and returned to me.

"Look, I know this isn't your ideal job. I wish I had a crystal ball for every time I was uncertain about my future, but you can't stay wound up as tight as a pig's tail. One of these days you're gonna scream and you won't be able to stop. And if you don't stop, those people in white coats will cart you away. And where will that leave Paisley?"

I didn't answer her because I didn't have an answer...at least not one she would want to hear.

"I'll work with you on the chickens. You have to get the hang of it for at least three or four days until I am able to move around better. We will go out together each day. But in regards to Paisley, you need...good grief, I don't know what you need. Just try getting to know your own daughter instead of distancing yourself from her. After all, you too just have each other."

I was so out of here. Once she was asleep, I'd wrap those leftovers in foil, chisel old meg from her limestone home, and be gone by three a.m. "I think I can do it with your help," I lied.

"Just don't kill my chickens. Now, go change out of that nasty shirt and come help me make supper."

Ironically, we had chicken and biscuits for supper, something I could easily wrap in foil and pack in my suitcase when we left that night. She cut the chicken in bite-size pieces for Paisley. Paisley mimicked Butterball's every move, even wiping her face with her napkin after she was done eating. Butterball praised her for everything she did. I couldn't remember the last time I told Paisley she had done something good. When Butterball offered to give her a bath, I immediately agreed.

KP duty wasn't hard, but the splashing and laughter that echoed into the kitchen made it obvious they were having more fun than I was. Like a moth to the flame, down the hallway I went.

"Where are your toes?" Paisley giggled in response to Butterball's question. "That's right. Where are your knees? Where is your tummy? Oh, Paisley is smart. Where is the water?" I heard splashing and giggling from behind the door.

"Where is your heart? Good. Where is my heart? That's right. You know your mama has a heart too, but sometimes I think she forgets where it is."

I retreated toward the living room as water drained from the tub. Moments later, she handed me Paisley wrapped in a towel. She quickly fell asleep after I dressed her in pajamas and tucked her in. I turned to leave the room and saw my reflection in the mirror. On my white T-shirt was a small, wet impression of Paisley's handprint over my heart. Of course, she couldn't have known what she was doing. Could she? This was Paisley after all, the toddler who still sucked on her toes. She was just holding on was all. She couldn't have known what Butterball was doing. She wasn't there mentally yet. She was just copying what Butterball did.

How could this woman have a connection with her in a matter of days, when it had taken me months to get where I was with her? It wasn't until I put my hand over her impression that I thought we might need to stay just a little longer. When I

61

pulled my jeans off to get pajamas on too, a coin fell out. George Washington stared at me. "Okay, Georgie. Do we stay or do we go?" I tossed the coin and caught it on the back of my arm. "Heads, we stay. Tails, we leave." I lifted my fingers slowly, and Georgie's head glistened in the overhead light.

Then Butterball bellowed, "Tess, can you come here?"

I sulked into the kitchen, feeling ten years old again, after Dad had found my report card in the garbage.

"I need your help for a minute." Her voice strained as she hovered over the kitchen sink. Her face red with a bead of sweat covering her upper lip. *Oh, please don't have a heart attack. I really can't handle anyone else dying on me.*

"What's wrong?"

"My ring. It's gone," she whispered as she stared down the drain.

Call it a freak talent, but I've always been able to unclog a drain. Once word got around my neighborhood back home in Alabama, I was unclogging drains and discovering treasure troves. My dad made me start charging twenty dollars for each visit. He said that was pennies compared to what a plumber would charge, and if I was going to pull out someone else's nasty leftovers, I should be compensated with more than a thank you. I made good money too.

"Get a bucket and a wrench. I got this covered," I smiled.

"What?"

"You heard me. I'm going to get your ring."

Butterball scurried to the utility room and came back with a bucket and several wrenches of various sizes. All items from underneath the sink were tossed on the kitchen floor as I crawled under and turned on my back, facing the piping.

"You really think you can get it?" she asked as she handed me the bucket with shaking hands.

This was simple enough. She had a P-trap. I'll bet it was in there—a pearl sitting in an oyster waiting to be opened. In my best doctor imitation, I thrust my hand upward and said, "Wrench."

The operation commenced. Butterball sat on the floor and watched me anxiously.

"I first met him when I was twenty-one."

"Who?" I asked as I briefly looked at her.

"Simon," she whispered. "My husband was the kindest, gentlest, and most giving man I have ever met." Her voice had taken on a softer tone. "His eyes showed everything he felt and thought. When he looked at me the first time with those deep-set brown eyes, I knew he had fallen in love with me. He walked up to me—a complete stranger—and asked me to marry him. I laughed in his face. Six months later, on our wedding night, I apologized for that. Many women were swooning over him, but he only had eyes for me. I never understood why. Geez, look at me—overweight, frizzy hair, crooked teeth—I didn't give a flip about fashion. When I pointed it out, he said, 'Exactly. You're real. No pretense or makeup to hide who you really are. You're who I've been looking for. Looks change. Personality doesn't.' I realized I better marry this one even though he was as crazy as a loon. I wasn't going to find another man even remotely as amazing as he was. I could either wait until I was skinny and dressed for the catwalk, or go for it and enjoy my fried chicken too. He taught me to love...me." Butterball smiled.

"The ring you are looking for is my wedding band. He gave me two beautiful children before he died of pneumonia in my arms. Our children live far away. He said all he needed was for me to hold him and that would heal him. What a crock, huh? Do you know what it's like to hold someone and feel them take their last breath? You have to find that ring, Tess," she ordered.

"You mean this ring?" I announced and handed her a slimy gold ring with threads of food hanging on it. The remaining gunk fell with a loud plop from the pipe. It resembled a hairball.

She screamed loud enough that I jumped and hit my head on the overhead pipe. By the time I put the pipe together and stood up, the ring was home again on the chubby finger of her left hand.

"I know it's silly of me to still wear this on my left hand seeing as how I'm a widow. It just seemed so final to keep it in the jewelry box. It sure is beautiful, isn't it?" she said as she shoved it in my face with leftover tidbits stuck in the setting.

Who was I to ruin the moment and mention it? "Yep, it sure is pretty."

We exchanged goodnights, and she disappeared into her bedroom. I cleaned up again, slipped into my pajamas, and slid under the covers. These were definitely not twenty-five-count sheets. That alone should keep me here for a while. Paisley giggled in her sleep for a few moments, and the entire house fell silent except for the faint, soothing sound of Butterball snoring from across the house.

I guess there are good guys still out there, somewhere among all the Thom's. There might be hope for me yet. A vision of male and female worms dancing with tiaras on their heads was the last thing I remember before I dozed off.

***

The next several days were less dramatic as Butterball taught me everything I needed to know to work solo during her recovery week. She showed me photos from the last few Worm Grunting Festivals. Flyers were posted all over town about the upcoming event. The most exciting topic of conversation I heard in town was that the currently reigning Worm Grunting Queen might have competition. I never would have thought that would be a coveted title, but these little old ladies took it seriously.

Butterball and I decided to trade skills, basic plumbing in exchange for cooking lessons. I think I fared better. Her first time disconnecting the pipes under the sink resulted in water in her face. A wet Butterball ain't a happy Butterball.

"I'll just have to superglue the ring on my finger," she said as she wiped her face clean.

"Think of it as a puzzle. You just have to figure out how to put all the pieces together," I explained.

"At least you know how to cook now," Butterball said. "When I have my surgery on Friday, I expect chicken and dumplings with homemade biscuits for supper."

The grocery store around the corner was having a sale on canned chicken and dumplings. Buy one, get one free. I made a mental note to get a few.

"Have you noticed that Paisley is trying to walk? She's been holding onto the walls with one hand now. Her balance is improving. I'll bet any day now she will walk."

"Don't hold your breath," I mumbled to myself but forced a smile for Butterball.

Paisley had become an algae eater again with her face smashed against the window, watching the waves outside. It could be months before she walked without holding onto anything, if she walked at all.

"I think you underestimate her," Butterball said. "She'll do it in her own time."

"Are you packed for your hospital trip?" I changed the subject.

She rolled her eyes and walked away. "Yes, Mother."

Her surgery was just two days away. I was nervous about taking care of her but tried not to let it show. I hoped it wouldn't bring back more memories of taking care of Dad, memories that I wished I could erase.

I joined Paisley at the window, and we both became algae eaters. With the sun setting over the water, colors of sherbet orange, golden yellow, and burnt red spanned the sky for as far as I could see. For a world with such a vast amount of space above, I sure felt claustrophobic where I was. I scooped Paisley up in my arms.

"We're turning in for the night," I said and retreated quickly to my side of the house.

CHAPTER EIGHT

I'm not sure what woke me up, but something didn't feel right. Normally, the house was quiet, except for Butterball's snoring from across the house, but I was sure that I heard someone in the kitchen. Paisley's small body, the size of a small cat, was curled up underneath the baby blanket. She slept peacefully, undisturbed by what I heard. I focused on the sounds coming from the kitchen as a warm, yellow glow crept under my bedroom door. Butterball had probably gone into the kitchen for one of her midnight raids. The resonating sound of Butterball snoring, mixed with the squeaky hinge on the kitchen cabinet, caught my attention.

Someone was in the house. I bolted out of the bed and scanned the dark room for something—anything—with which to protect myself, Paisley, and Butterball.

A memory of Dad straddled over a burglar in our house came to mind. I would have slept through the entire incident if not for the guy screaming like a little girl when Dad caught him. I recalled my dad's swearing was comparable to a drill sergeant as he barked orders to him. I had never heard him that angry before. Curiosity had gotten the best of me, and I tiptoed out of my bedroom to find Dad crouching over a skinny kid with greasy hair. Dad saw me staring and yelled at me to call the police. They arrived in ten minutes and carted the burglar away. My dad was still red-faced even after they left. He hugged me and said we were safe, and he would never let anyone hurt me. I sure wish he was here now.

Maybe it was a homeless person looking for food in the pantry. Couldn't the burglar see the live chickens outside, take them, and just leave? They wouldn't really be missed. I'd be glad they were gone. One less beak to feed. *Okay, Tess, refocus here.* I needed something big, hard, and sharp. Feeling around in the dark in an unfamiliar room wasn't fun. My hands landed on a hairbrush on the top of the dresser. Sure, there was a novel idea. I could threaten him with split ends. My other choice was one of Paisley's shoes that I'd left on the dresser. Perfect, if I was killing a spider. My fingers closed around a cold, glass bottle of perfume. Closest thing to mace a woman can get in a predicament such as this.

I opened the door slowly and tiptoed down the hallway. A woman's figure stood in the kitchen. Her back was to me as she faced the counter, left of the stove. I snuck up to just two feet away, raised the perfume to face level. Primed and ready to relinquish this venom, I did my best Amazon warrior's yell. When she whipped around, all I saw was the kitchen light glistening off a massive butcher knife. A spasm caused my trigger finger to twitch, and I instantly felt my eyes catch fire. I screamed and crumpled like the witch in the *Wizard of Oz*. I couldn't believe the searing pain as my eyes melted in their sockets.

"What the hell is going on out here?" asked Butterball as she rushed out of her room. "And why does it smell like an Avon store?"

"She sprayed her eyes with perfume," the intruder said in a familiar voice.

Butterball and the intruder led me to the bathroom where they flushed my eyes with cold water.

"I thought you weren't due back until next week?" Butterball asked.

"Dirk called me and said that you had a temporary roommate, and he wanted me to make sure you were okay," said the other woman.

"Oh, that. She won't be here long. We're working on a trade. She will cover all photo shoots for me while I recover from surgery. And I offered her and her daughter a room and food in exchange. It's a win-win, huh?"

"She has a daughter too? How about twins, Butterball. Does she have a boyfriend in the back room too?"

"Nope, that's all."

Finally, my eyes stopped melting, and I was handed a towel to dry my face. I cracked my swollen eyelids and looked around. Everything was still blurry, but at least they weren't on fire anymore. I rubbed my eyes and tried to focus. When I looked up again, I couldn't believe what I saw. The meat cleaver-yielding woman was Gabrielle Stone, my best friend— or maybe I should say ex-best friend—from high school.

Just my luck to have traces of my hometown right here. Her eyes squinted in suspicion when she recognized me. She stepped forward, just inches from my face.

"Hi."

"Hi, back," I said being a smart ass.

"Been a long time, Tess."

"Sure has," I answered. We stared at each other in silence.

"Watch out for the sagebrush," Butterball said as she cut the tension. "Are y'all about to have a shoot-out?"

Gabs cut her eyes over to Butterball. "We go back a little ways."

I stood there, unsure what to do. Do I pack up and leave tonight? Where do I go from here?

Gabs was the girl who everyone teased in high school, but she didn't care. She proudly strutted around in her zebra-striped high tops and peacock earrings. She must have seen me as a pathetic, weak excuse for a girl who cowered at the first stare. I'm sure she used me as a science project for extra credit.

Her first words to me were, "You gonna eat your orange?" as I was leaving the lunch line with my tray. I offered it to her, too scared to say no. She took it and followed me to an empty

69

table, and we quickly became friends. I confided in her about my dad's illness. Just when I thought I had a true friend, she came to school one day and withdrew. She said her grandfather passed away in Colorado, and she and her family moved there to take care of his estate.

I'd just found out I was pregnant by Thom the day before and needed someone to talk to when she dropped a bomb on me. I never did tell her. After she left, I was invisible again, until I started showing, and then Paisley was born. I didn't know anyone in Florida, but since a dark cloud followed me, I thought moving to the Sunshine State would rid me of it.

Gabs's hair was more blonde than I remembered. Golden highlights framed her face. Over two years had passed since we last saw each other, but in my heart, it was an eternity. So much in my life was different now, things of which she knew nothing, and apparently her wardrobe had changed in hers. She wore a white tank top, khaki pants, and old, dirty work boots. Her hair was pulled into a haphazard bun at the nape of her neck with golden tendrils falling around her face.

"Tess Cooper. Unbelievable," she said shaking her head. "Are you enjoying your stay in my house?"

"Your house? I thought it was Butterball's niece's house." I looked at Butterball, confused and embarrassed.

"I'm the *niece*. I own it. Part of my grandfather's estate. The reason I left, remember?"

I remembered all too well, but I was tired and done with this. "Oh, I had forgotten," I lied. "Nice place you have here." I tried to change the conversation, but Paisley cried out. I headed for the bedroom, leaving Butterball and Gabs in the bathroom. When I returned with Paisley in my arms, they were in a heated discussion in the living room.

"I'll pack and be out of here tonight." I figured it would cool their tempers since I knew the argument was about me.

"What? I still need you to help with the Worm Grunting Festival. Gabrielle doesn't know a camera lens from a contact lens. You can't just leave me two days before my surgery," Butterball pleaded.

Gabs scoffed at Butterball's remark. "Look, we weren't talking about you. I was irritated that she didn't call to tell me about her surgery, so I could cut my trip early and be here for her. You being here doesn't bother me in the least. Matter of fact, I feel better with Butterball having someone here. It keeps her from getting into trouble." Gabs gave Butterball a lopsided grin.

Her tone changed instantly when she looked back at me, "But we have unfinished business, don't we?"

Paisley wiggled and turned to face her. Gabs's face changed, and I knew she saw something different in Paisley's appearance.

"We *definitely* have unfinished business," she replied.

"Well, on that note, I am going back to bed," Butterball said. "Please put the perfume bottle back on the dresser. It is discontinued, and I don't want to waste it. Gabby girl, throw her in the chicken coop if she pisses you off. She is afraid of them. I've wanted to do it at least six times already since she's been here. Tess, just call her a boney-assed, bleach blonde. It will send her over the edge. At least it does when I say it. Goodnight, girls." We watched Butterball return to the back bedroom.

"Butterball, where are you going?" asked Gabs.

"Oh, come on." Butterball stamped her foot. "It's the middle of the night. I already have drool on your pillow cases and have been sleeping naked on your sheets. You really don't want to go in there tonight. Just let me catch a few more hours of sleep, and I'll move back to my room tomorrow night," she pleaded.

"I really didn't need the visual. Fine," Gabs said, and then she turned to me. "Now is as good a time as any to talk," she said as she pulled a couple of old quilts from the hall closet and laid them on the floor. "Your daughter can nap on the quilt.

Have a seat." She patted the couch beside her. I laid Paisley gently down on the pink and white pinwheel quilt, brushed invisible dust off of it, fluffed it, fiddled with her pajamas, and moved a few strands of hair from her face. I wasn't ready to be interrogated.

"Do you think she might want a massage and a tattoo while I wait?"

Time to face the interrogator. "Well, at least I know you're still a smart ass. Okay, what do you want to know? I'm an open book."

"More in the making of a deadbolt diary, but I'm pretty good at picking locks," she said with a smile.

***

Two pots of coffee and an entire cheesecake later, we were still talking when Butterball emerged bleary-eyed. She grabbed a cup of coffee, scratched her ass, and disappeared into the back bedroom.

"Paisley went without a name for a couple of days. I chose her name because the head nurse brought her to me in a green, paisley baby blanket that was donated to the nursery unit. A nurse started calling her 'Miss Paisley,' and it just sorta stuck. Her middle name came from the nurse's name tag. Renee," I said with a blank stare.

"I had no idea you went through so much after I left," she said with sagging shoulders.

"That's nothing compared to when I was released from the hospital with her. I've never babysat a day in my life. I'm an only child. I've never even had a pet to take care of." I paced while Paisley slept peacefully.

"I had a baby doll once that Dad gave me at Christmas when I was six. I named her Doll. Again, that should have been a clue that I wasn't meant to have children. I left her on a school playground when her hair got stuck in the chains of the swing set. I was mad at her for letting that happen, so I left her there to teach her a lesson. When I went back the next day, she was gone. All that remained were some wiry, blonde hairs entwined in the chains." Gabs giggled.

"You see, these are the things I should have told Nurse Renee!" I said exasperated. "Look at the mess I'd gotten myself into nine months earlier. I couldn't take care of myself, let alone a baby. I totally winged it with my dad, and you now know how that turned out."

"Look, you can't blame yourself for what happened to him. That is something entirely different. No one could have done any better than you did, considering the circumstances you were dealt. Good grief, you were not even an adult yet."

Her words did little to comfort me. "What I didn't know was that Dad had been fighting cancer for several months before I told him I was pregnant. He kept it from me. He was hoping to beat it, but he became one of those stick figures that little kids draw in school. He lost sixty pounds, Gabrielle! And you know what he said when I told him I was pregnant?" She shook her head. "He said not to worry because we would all be fine. He lied! He left me alone with a baby, and he lied." I ended it with a whisper.

"And you will be fine. Don't you see? You've made it this far. Paisley is still breathing, and her hair isn't tangled in a park swing."

"Did I tell you Social Services tried to place us in a foster home? No one wants a seventeen-year-old with a disabled newborn. They tried contacting people out of state, but no one was interested in taking us in together. I think they dragged their feet though. I'm sure they secretly wanted me to age out so they could just place Paisley. We left before they could get her. I sold Dad's trailer, pulled my savings of six hundred seventy-one dollars and forty-two cents and left." I sunk down beside Gabs on the couch. She touched my hand, and I jerked it away. I slowly turned to her and began to whisper, ashamed of the words coming out. I didn't want Paisley to hear them, even though I knew she wouldn't understand them.

"I seriously considered letting Social Services take her. Life would have been much easier going solo," I said as I looked down at my trembling hands. Dad would have been disappointed with me if I did that. It's the only reason she is still with me. Well, that and the fact that I needed someone to talk to. I kept those thoughts to myself. Gabs tried to console me with words, but I didn't hear them as I continued to ramble.

"I remember not long after she was born, sitting on the floor in the corner of my room, holding her in my arms, and crying as quietly as I could, so I wouldn't wake up Dad."

Gabs stood up. "Tess, you know your dad loved her even though she's disabled. I'm sure it didn't matter to him."

"He never knew," I said as Gabs's eyes widened in shock. "He never knew she has Down syndrome. He was heavily medicated. He knew she was born, but I kept her covered with blankets and he never really saw her full in the face to see her features."

"I don't understand. Why didn't you tell him?" she asked, stunned.

"Why should I?" I stated matter-of-fact. "He couldn't change her. He couldn't make the bridge of her nose normal, her tongue smaller, and her brain smarter. He couldn't make himself better. No. He didn't need to know. He needed rest. And while he slept, I cried enough for all of us."

She grabbed me and hugged me tight. When she pulled back, tears were running down her cheeks. "I'm sorry. I had no idea. I tried to call a few times, but you were never home. I wrote, but you never wrote back. Matter of fact, all my letters came back as 'undeliverable.' I assumed you moved. You know I would have come back to help, if I'd known."

"I was pissed at you, Gabs. You abandoned me! I received those letters and sent them all back. I was standing beside my dad when he told you I wasn't home, just as I begged him to. I was done with everything and everyone. Admit it. You wouldn't have come back if you'd known," I said and patted her on the leg. "You had your own life." I smiled weakly.

"Well, if I couldn't have helped with Paisley, I would have at least rearranged a few faces of the kids at school for what they put you through, especially Thom's. I knew he was bad news the moment I met him our senior year."

"Funny, I've known him since kindergarten and didn't see it, huh?"

"I did come back, you know."

"What?"

"From what I can guess, it was maybe about a month after you left. Everyone clammed up when I asked about you and your dad. I was told about your dad but not Paisley. It wasn't until I went to put flowers on his grave that I ran into your old neighbor, Jane Neel. She told me about you being pregnant and Paisley being born," Gabs said. "So, let me get this straight. Thom abandoned you, you had a baby born with a handicap, and your dad died all in the same year." Gabs glimpsed at Paisley nestled on the quilt as she made fish lips while sleeping. She hugged me again. "You're not alone anymore."

I buried my face in her shoulder and felt an emotional wave crash down on me.

"My deodorant is over twenty-four hours old, and it promised twelve-hour protection. Don't take a deep breath down there, okay?"

My voice was muffled by her shoulder, but she still heard me. "I don't understand why everyone keeps leaving me. Am I an awful person? Maybe it is a good thing Paisley has a handicap. She'll never leave me because she will need me. Oh, my gosh! I can't believe I just said that." I buried my face deeper into her shoulder and discovered she was right about the deodorant, but I didn't care at that point.

"I'm sure I still have red clay on my high heels from the funeral. I can't even look at those heels. I tossed them in the back seat of Dad's car after the funeral and haven't pulled them out since."

"Just leave those red clay memories behind."

I started to cry. I hadn't cried since Alabama. I'd just been angry. This wasn't a little sob either. It was a tsunami. I cried so hard that I ended up on the floor in the bathroom throwing up all the cheesecake. My head rested on my forearm as it lay across the cold, porcelain toilet bowl, and I stared at the clear water below. Gabs came into the bathroom and sat on the side of the tub.

"Sorry about throwing up. I'll clean up anything that didn't make it in the toilet," I offered, my voice echoing in the toilet bowl.

"Don't worry about it. A clean toilet is never a permanent thing anyway." She nudged me playfully. We both giggled, and I sat up facing her.

"I think I've been holding that in for quite a while."

"Glad you finally got it out, the crying…and the cheesecake. You know, it will go to your hips." I went to hug her, and she fanned her face and pointed toward the mouthwash. I swished some in my mouth and spit it in the toilet.

"I think I'll just sip on water," I said as we strolled toward the kitchen. She reached for the butcher knife she had in her hand the previous night.

"Don't worry. I'm more of a Betty Crocker than a serial killer," she teased. "I was chopping carrots to snack on later today, but I think they are a little stale now." She tossed the partially cut carrots in the trash and placed the knife in the sink.

"Well, I guess I could make us something to eat since you have more room now." She winked. "Unless you want to go for breakfast."

"What about Paisley?" I looked at her still slumbering on the quilt.

"I'll get Butterball to watch her." She disappeared into her bedroom and came out two minutes later. "Change her diaper, put her in the crib, and get dressed. Butterball will be out in a few minutes."

I washed my face, changed clothes, and forty-five minutes later we sat eating breakfast at Myra Jean's.

I looked up at Gabs between sips of orange juice. A devilish smile slowly stretched across her face. "Are you interested in learning what happened to Thom after you left?" she asked.

I'd thought of him often. Most of the thoughts were of him mutilated in some manner or sort. Maybe stranded in the Apalachicola National Forest next to a bear den with nothing covering his body but a thick layer of sticky honey. Winnie the Pooh, where are you? I'd make sure he had good running shoes on. I'm not heartless.

"Nope. Not at all," I answered.

"You're lying. I might have known you for just part of our senior year, but you've never been good at lying. You have about ten seconds, and I'll never mention it again."

I took another bite of my bacon, "Please tell me he lost all his teeth, lost his gorgeous curly locks, has twelve children by twelve different women, is paying alimony out of his ass, sells turnips and collards out of the back of his pickup, and lives on Ramen noodles."

She leaned forward and rested on her forearms. "Better," she said, and paused for effect. I kicked her under the table to get her to continue and shoved the last bit of biscuit in my mouth.

"He *was* working at a convenience store but has spent the last six months in prison for grand theft. He was pulled over for expired tags. During a search of his car, the cops found a trunk full of women's undergarments from one of those fancy high dollar department stores at the mall with tags still intact, but no receipts. The garments were valued at over five thousand dollars."

I choked the last bite of my biscuit down. "That's awful...ly wonderful," I said and smiled.

"There's more."

"More?" I stared at her in fascination as if her words became the cream filling of a pastry.

"When he was pulled over, he was *wearing* some of the underwear," she said with a smirk. "Word around town was that it was fishnet stockings with edible panties." She smiled satisfied. "Ain't you glad he left you?"

"Now I am," I answered. All traces of wanting Thom back in my life vanished that very morning in Myra Jean's in the second booth to the right, just under the window. For the first time since Paisley's birth, I was going to take one step forward. My life was better without Thom. Paisley's life would be better without Thom. He made me look good.

Gabs brought me back to the present. "I noticed when we left the house that you had your dad's Thunderbird. I didn't recognize it last night. You know, Dirk, our local mechanic can fix it up for you. Make it more dependable. That thing is about to fall apart."

My mood took a turn to the dark side. "I met Dirk, and no, thank you."

She ignored my comment. "Do you remember all those times you would sneak out of the house, and we would take that Bird for a ride down Bearden Boulevard to hoot and holler at the cute guys? We always stopped at a car wash on the way home and vacuumed out the Cheetos, so your dad wouldn't have an aneurysm. Oh, my gosh! I completely forgot about the squirrel you ran over two blocks from your house. Do you think the Popsicle stick cross we made is still standing where we buried that thing?" Gabs looked as if she was seriously considering the chances of that thing still standing upright.

The thought of roadkill was ruining my appetite. "Enough about me. We've been talking about me since last night. What have you been doing since we last saw each other?"

She leaned back in the vinyl seat as if getting ready to tell a grand story. "Well, after Granddaddy died and left the beach house to me, I pretty much just enjoyed the sunsets for a while." She shoved her plate to the center of the table and turned her utensils face down on it. "Oh, and I got my GED." She pulled her hair over one shoulder and started making a braid while talking.

"The beach house had been empty for a couple of decades and needed repairs. With the help of local volunteers, it didn't take much to fix it up. I enrolled in college and volunteered on an archaeological dig just for fun when I was bored one Saturday. I fell in love with the professor and archaeology," she said with a smile. "We have been dating and digging since, all around Wakulla County."

"I noticed the fireplace. Was that his handy work?"

"Yep. I'm loving that meg tooth. I still can't believe we found that in a slab of limestone. Oh, I've taken up scuba diving too." She paused as if reflecting. "I haven't yet been able to find a zebra-striped scuba suit though."

Flashbacks of her zebra-striped high tops danced in my head. We both laughed at the recollection.

"Shopping. Shopping is what we need to do to burn off this breakfast," she said as she paid our bill.

"Gabs. I don't have the money to shop. I'm almost tapped out as it is," I whispered in embarrassment.

"Didn't I tell you? This is National Find a Homeless Girl, Buy Her Breakfast, and Take Her Shopping Day. Tess, you're very lucky. Not many people observe this day," she said as she slapped me on the ass.

CHAPTER NINE

After strolling through the mall in Tallahassee for four hours, I found a few cheap blouses. She brought me pants to try on while I was in a dressing room.

"Good grief, Tess. Are you wearing Butterball's underwear?" she teased, as she peeked over the curtain.

"No," I said in defense of my high-top briefs. "They're just…comfortable."

"Comfortable enough to play bingo at the old folks' home. You need sexy underwear, not nursing home underwear."

I looked at myself in the mirror. Stark-white, high-top briefs covered the stretch marks on my belly, and rose about two inches above my navel. "I'm fine in these. I feel…safe."

"Damn straight. Ain't nobody gonna try to break into your pants with you wearing a diaper," she quipped. She stood there with the dressing room curtain ajar and one hand on her hip. Two women stole glimpses over her shoulder and giggled.

"Fine," I said. "We can go to another department store and—"

She shook her head and finger at me. "You buy tools and household appliances at other department stores. Not underwear," she spouted off. "Get dressed. I'll take you where I shop."

She paid for my blouses, and I was dragged to Chantilly's Boudoir, an upscale women's boutique for the rich and skinny…both of which I wasn't.

Paisley Memories | Zelle Andrews

I dug the heels of my sneakers in the floor to stop us. "Oh, no. Nothing will fit me in here." I resisted, but she tightened her grip on my forearm and pulled me through the door, right past the size-zero mannequins with their erect nipples poking through the sheer material, like a lighthouse during a storm, to alert all men within a one-mile radius of where the hot girls would be shopping. All hot girls, except me.

I noticed three preteen boys standing across from the store, gawking at the mannequins while holding their sodas and trying to look inconspicuous. They weren't fooling anyone.

"It's not supposed to fit. It's supposed to look sexy," she said and rolled her eyes at me while thumbing through a display of undies.

"How about these?" she asked as she held up a piece of red lace that would have fit the baby doll I abandoned at the park.

"Um, let me think about it," I said as I placed a finger aside my face and pretended I was seriously considering this. "No!"

She tossed the red undies back and held a white lace thong across her pelvis and jiggled her hips. "These?"

I was exasperated. "The difference is that those are white." I glimpsed over my shoulder, and the boys were still there, but this time their eyes moved from the mannequins to Gabs as she swiveled her hips in a playful mood. She was oblivious to the boys.

"Well, since you are acting all innocent, I thought you might want them." She tossed them down and grabbed an apricot thong with sequins around the waist. "Keep looking. I'm going to try and find more like these."

Several pairs had sheer material with the solid part being a heart the size of a thumbnail to cover the privates. I passed on those too. The boys ventured closer to the entrance of the store. With wide eyes, they took in all that they could see. Were they hoping to see something more? I'm glad I wasn't born a boy.

"Do you have any *real* underwear?" I asked a size-two employee.

81

"Are you looking for something for your mother or grandmother?" she asked with a smile.

"Why, yes, I am."

"Try on the other side of the mall." She quickly turned on her stiletto heels and marched her size-two ass to the next paying customer. Seconds later, I was blindfolded with material. I yanked it off, and in my hands was a zebra-striped, lace thong.

"Too bad you don't still have your zebra-striped high tops," I said.

"These aren't for me. They are for you."

"Absolutely not," I answered.

"You are so frigid. I'm surprised you had a baby." She tore the undies from my hands and paid for several undergarments that she picked up. As the stiletto queen gave Gabs her credit card back, she looked sideways at me. "Sorry about that comment. It was mean, but you have to do something just for fun, even if you are the only one who ever sees them."

"I really think I will be more comfortable taking care of a baby in granny panties rather than a thong, thank you. I'll see you in the food court." Before I stormed off, I caught the pathetic look of the stiletto queen as she silently pointed her boney finger in the direction I should go to find those granny panties. I passed the three boys on the way out. They surrounded the mannequin. One of them reached with shaking hands to touch the plastic, erect nipple of the mannequin. His fingers, a mere inch away. The tip of his finger just touched Mt. Everest when—

"Donald Hubert Kherrigan the third! Get your butt over here!" yelled a woman about Butterball's age from halfway across the mall. They jumped and ran to the woman. She smacked all three on the back of their heads as they lined up behind her to follow. They gave each other high fives of approval and fell in line. Again, I'm glad I wasn't born a boy.

We purchased drinks and settled into a couple of metal chairs in front of an enormous water fountain situated between two sets of escalators. The water spewed over twenty feet high and came down with a loud roar. Silver and copper-colored coins covered the bottom of the fountain. We watched without exchanging words.

As I was about to ask Gabs if she was ready to leave, a young woman and her daughter sat down at the table next to us. They both wore baseball caps and laughed about a private conversation between themselves. While the mother settled down in the chair, the daughter walked toward the fountain with her hand cupped. She closed her eyes, and I watched as she mouthed a private wish and then tossed several coins into the water.

"What did you wish for?" asked the mother.

"If I tell you, it won't come true. Remember?" answered the young girl.

"That doesn't count for moms. Come on. I want to know," her mother coaxed.

The young girl rolled her eyes. "I wished Jasper was here," she said with a gleam in her eyes.

Her mother smiled and looked over her daughter's shoulder. "Well, what do you know? I think your wish came true," she said.

The young girl whipped off her baseball cap and whirled around to see who was approaching them. I saw her full in the face. She had the unmistakable features of someone with Down syndrome. My heart froze as I watched her jump up, nearly knocking over her chair, as she sprinted to the boy who was obviously her boyfriend. Her boyfriend, Jasper, had Down syndrome too. They hugged each other and shared a bird peck. He sat down with the couple and shared french fries with his girlfriend. I wanted to talk to the mom but didn't know how to start. A million questions raced in my head, but I couldn't get them past my lips. It was too late to ask them as I watched the love-birds walk away holding hands, and I imagined Cupid hearts shooting to the moon and back above their heads.

Time to make a wish, I thought as I shoved my hands deep in my pockets and came up with lint and the wheat penny that belonged to my dad. He gave it to me shortly before he died. He'd said he found it the day he fell in love with my mother. He carried it everywhere as he said it brought him luck. Well, it hadn't worked for me yet. Maybe this would help.

Could it really be as easy as throwing it in the fountain and making a wish? It worked for the young woman, so why not me? What would I wish for? A life without Paisley? A life with Paisley but without Down syndrome and her toe-sucking addiction? A life with my dad again. A life in which I ran like my pants were on fire in kindergarten when Thom smiled at me the first time. Everything I thought of either sounded selfish or stupid. I balled up my fist with the copper coin, holding it high and felt it getting warm from my sweaty palm. I was just about to hurl it with all my strength when a hand closed over my fist.

"Wish for happiness and laughter. That is all you need," Gabs whispered into my ear.

I squeezed my eyes tight and made the wish that would seal my fate as it had for the young couple walking away hand in hand. "I wish for happiness and laughter." The penny rose high. The lights glistened off of it as it rolled in the air. A baby squealed, causing me to look away for a moment, just long enough that I missed seeing it fall into the bubbling water. I'm sure it landed, but not seeing it land bothered me. I waited to feel different, but I felt the same.

"Stupid magic fountain," I said and let out a long, deep sigh.

"Wishes don't always happen instantaneously," Gabs said. "Let's head home. You can model your new undies for Butterball."

At that moment, I thought maybe I should have wished those panties away.

CHAPTER TEN

When we pulled into the driveway, something didn't look right. Gabs parked her car in the very spot I had parked my car. My car was gone. I lunged from Gabs's car before it was completely stopped.

"Where is my car?" I asked as calmly as I could. She didn't answer. "Where is my car?" I yelled.

She gathered our bags and rushed to the end of the driveway to stand beside me. I ran down the street, past two houses and back. Gabs followed me, the plastic shopping bags crinkling in her hands. When I finally stopped, she came to stand beside me again, heaving as she tried to catch her breath.

"Geez, this must be how Butterball feels. Bless her heart," she said, and her eyes got huge with panic. "Please don't tell her I said that. She will beat me until I resemble a scrambled egg."

"Who would steal an old, rusted Thunderbird?" I asked as I raced back to where my car had been parked. I searched for tracks, but there was nothing to find when it comes to broken shells for a driveway. I went to the end of the driveway, which was more sand than shells, but there were many car tracks, and they all crisscrossed over each other. I stormed into the house and slammed the front door.

"Can you be any louder?" Gabs said as she opened the front door to let herself in.

"Oh, I can get louder all right. My car is gone. I need to call the police."

"What's going on?" Butterball emerged from the back porch with Paisley in her arms as I frantically dialed 9-1-1.

"Yes, Operator? Someone stole my car."

"Ma'am, 9-1-1 is for emergencies. You need to call the sheriff's office."

"This *is* an emergency. I'm homeless without it."

"Where are you calling from, ma'am?"

"I'm calling from my friends' house, as they've been letting me stay with them."

"You don't sound homeless to me, ma'am. Please call your sheriff's office to file a report." I heard a click.

"She hung up on me. She actually hung up on me." I slammed the receiver down. It didn't make me feel better, so I picked it up and slammed it down a few more times. When I looked up, Butterball's eyes were as round as pancakes, and Paisley stared with her mouth hanging open.

Gabs went to the refrigerator, took a magnet down, and handed it to me. "That is the number for the sheriff's office. Ask for Abby Sinclair. She's a friend."

"Does she work in the stolen car department?" I asked.

She rolled her eyes. "Just call that number."

I called the number and started blabbering the instant someone picked up the other end. "My car was stolen."

"What is your name, ma'am."

"Tess Cooper."

"Your address, ma'am."

"I think it's 2-3-0-1 Pelican Perch." I looked at Gabs, and she nodded.

I could hear her typing away on acrylic nails, and she paused when I said the address.

"Are you staying with Butterball...err, Naomi Mitchell and Gabrielle Stone?"

"Yes, ma'am. My car is a 1957 Thunderbird, and the license plate is—"

"I haven't seen Butterball in ages. How's she doing? The last time I saw her was at Pot Belly's bar in Sopchoppy. She won two hundred dollars on the pool table. Ha, I remember when—"

"Look, it's all nice and everything that you remember her, but I'm missing my car."

"Oh, right. Okay, sugar…err, ma'am. What is the make and model?"

I answered all her petty questions. Once she was done, I asked her a question. "When will I get my car back?"

"Ma'am, all I can do is file the report. Cross your fingers, toes, and eyes. And what the heck, rub your lucky rabbit's foot. With a little luck, it might just turn up."

"Okay, but when?" I persisted.

We can't put a time frame on this, ma'am. Unfortunately, there are a few chop shops around here."

"What's a chop shop?"

"It's where they break down your vehicle piece by piece and sell the parts for more money than they would get if they sold the entire car. But don't worry, sugar, there isn't a large market for Thunderbird parts down here. I'll bet some teenagers just took it for a joy ride."

"But I'm not getting any joy out of this," I spat back.

"Be sure to tell Butterball that Sinclair said hey." Then she hung up.

I slammed the phone down and then picked it up and slammed it down again a few times just for the pure joy of it.

"You're gonna have to buy Gabs a new phone if you keep that up," Butterball hollered from the living room. She was lounging on the couch with Paisley sitting in her lap. I shuffled to the couch and plopped my butt next to her. Paisley crawled into my lap and pulled herself up to stand on my thighs by grabbing my hair. As I pried her vice-grip fingers off and got her settled down, it started to really sink in. This time, I really was trapped. I couldn't go anywhere, even if I wanted to. I had almost no money, and now, no transportation. I'd just have to surrender and raise chickens with Butterball for the rest of my life. *Shoot me now, please.*

"I don't know what to do," I said in exasperation, as I slammed my head into the back of the couch.

"Let the police do their police thingy, and I'm sure it will show up," Butterball said with confidence.

I swallowed hard, "I'm going to need to help you a lot longer than expected, so I can get money to buy a new car. Do you think Gabs will mind me staying a little longer?"

"I think she would love that. My surgery is tomorrow. I would love to have someone at my beck and call for a while." Her eyes lit up. "Maybe Dirk can help you find a cheap car."

"Oh, what a novel idea. Get Dirk to help me. I quiver with anticipation." I faked a smile and hugged Paisley tighter.

"One more thing here. You really need to watch how you act around Paisley. Kids are sponges and mimic everything they see. She's going to start picking up your bad habits."

I pulled Paisley away from my chest and looked into her eyes. All I saw there was a vacant expression. "I don't think I need to worry," I retorted. Butterball glared at me, shaking her head.

"Did you hear me? I'm serious," Butterball insisted as I rolled my eyes. "If you were my daughter, I would get the 'hear me' stick on you," Butterball said with a smirk.

"What's that?" I asked innocently as Gabs sat down on the couch too.

Paisley lunged for her lap, and she scooped her up. "Oh, the almighty 'hear me' stick. I've felt the love from it a few times growing up." She laughed.

Now I was really interested in this stick. I looked at Butterball questioningly.

Butterball smiled and began her story. "The 'hear me' stick is just an ole four-foot yardstick that my dad bought at a hardware store and kept hanging in the hallway. When I misbehaved—which was at least once a week, if not more—he would tan my hide with it. While he was whipping my ample behind, he said, 'Do you hear me? Do you hear me now?' I always answered loud and clear so he would know I heard him. 'I hear ya. I hear ya.' I heard him loud and clear *that* week. His voice became sort of faint the next week when I found something else to do that was stupid."

Butterball excused herself to go to the bathroom but instead returned with the famous 'hear me' stick in her left hand. She patted the end of it against her leg making a smacking sound to get my attention.

I scooted to the edge of the couch, ready to spring. Butterball stared and her lower, right eyelid quivered. I envisioned sagebrush tumbling across the living room at high noon during our five-second showdown.

"You'd have to catch me first." I sprang from the couch and bolted away. She yelled a freakish war call and was after me.

My feet fumbled a couple steps as I ran out the front door and ducked down behind the trash can. I peeked around and didn't see her.

"Show yourself," I taunted.

Gabs came to the front door holding Paisley. "She didn't make it," she said and laughed. "She ran about ten feet and was laughing so hard she peed on herself. She ran to the bathroom instead, cussing."

We laughed with the seriousness of the situation temporarily matted down.

CHAPTER ELEVEN

"Rise and shine, sleepy head," Butterball said as she patted my rump to wake me up. "Dang girl, you been working out? Probably not. All young girls have tight buns. Hurry up and get dressed. We have to go. Let's get this thing outta me." She scooped up Paisley and took her to breakfast.

I jerked on black leggings, a white T-shirt, and black flip flops. No need to get dressed up if I'd be sitting on a vinyl chair in the waiting room. By the time I came out, Butterball and Paisley had finished breakfast, and Gabs emerged from her room—a ray of sunshine.

She wore the new sundress she had bought during our shopping expedition. There she stood in all her glory in a bright, canary-yellow sundress that flared out at the bottom, fifties style. Adorable silver sandals with rhinestones across the band adorned her feet. I suddenly felt that all I needed was a mop and a bucket of water, and I'd be ready to clean the floor.

She sensed how I felt. "You look fine. I wanted to wear it, that's all." She twirled around and the hem flared out.

"Okay, Fraulein Marie, go eat something so we can go," said Butterball.

We ate quickly and headed to Dirk's to drop off Paisley.

"Are you sure this is a good idea? I mean, I could take her with us," I offered, knowing the idea would be rejected.

"Paisley will be fine," Gabs said. "Dirk's wife helps with the childcare center occasionally. Plus, she has two kids of her own, remember? Besides, I need your help. This is Butterball we are talking about. She is a handful even when *not* medicated."

"I heard that," Butterball said as she smacked the back of Gabs's headrest.

***

My back was getting stiff as we sat in the waiting room during Butterball's gallbladder surgery. The only reading material available were sports and hunting magazines, two of which I had never heard of until that morning. While reading an article on tennis, I felt hot breath on my cheek. The man next to me leaned over, so he could see Kate Upton in a bikini on the next page. Her highlighted hair appeared to blow in a breeze as she stood ankle deep in beach water. I bristled and tilted my head in the opposite direction.

"Sorry," he mumbled.

I handed him the magazine. "That's okay. I was done with it anyway."

"Thanks." He happily took it and didn't turn the page for about two minutes. When his wife was pushed out in a wheelchair, he abruptly tossed it in my lap and jumped to her aid.

Finally, we were able to go back and see Butterball in recovery.

"She has to urinate prior to dismissal," a nurse explained. "She's been in the bathroom for over twenty minutes. Sometimes it takes the bladder a little bit of time to wake up after sedation."

Gabs knocked on the bathroom door. "How you doing in there?"

"You'd think the pressure would make my bladder rip apart. Give me another minute. I'm going to try something." We heard her turn the faucet on. "Whoa, this water is cold. Oh, yeah, here we go. It's raining in Kansas!"

Once Butterball was dressed, we were ready to go. She kept talking about this woman named Diane.

"Does Butterball know anyone named Diane?" I asked.

"I've never heard her talk about anyone named Diane," answered Gabs. We helped Butterball get in the wheelchair to be escorted out.

"You find that Diane! I'll show her how to insert an IV. I'll insert it right up her—"

"Butterball!" Gabs interrupted.

"Yep, right up her Butterball. That's a good place to stick it."

Butterball grabbed the straw out of her Styrofoam cup she had been given and handed it to Gabs. "Here are the keys. Now go get my unicorn, so we can get the hell out of here." She grabbed her own breast. "Do they look bigger to you? Cool."

We both looked at Butterball with her glassy eyes and knew we were in trouble. She had the same look on her face as my neighbors' cat when he came home neutered.

"Are you sure she shouldn't stay a little longer?" I asked.

"She can't, Tess. We need to get her home before she creates more of a scene. This is as good as it gets. We just can't let her see Diane. She can just sit in the car with you while I run into the drug store to get her prescription."

A nurse walked by, and Gabs grabbed her arm. Her name tag said "Diane," and Gabs quickly ripped it from her white blouse.

"Nurse *Delores*, we're good to go, right?"

The nurse stared in horror at her ripped blouse, but saw that Butterball was with us, so she partially shielded her face. "She could have left yesterday, for all I care."

"See, she is fine," Gabs said. I looked down at a river of spittle as it flowed from the corner of Butterball's mouth.

"We can sit in the car right? You'll be fast, right?" I asked as stress kicked in.

"My nickname is Flash Gordon," she answered.

Butterball screamed, "Ahh ahh."

The nurse pushed her to our car and practically dumped her in the back seat like manure out of a wheel barrel.

I attempted to fasten the seat belt around Butterball as carefully as I could so that I didn't hurt her stomach. She grabbed my face.

"Better sit down. I hear Space Mountain is a really fast rollercoaster."

"Just sit in the back seat with her to calm her down," Gabs said.

Three tries later and I still couldn't get the seat belt fastened. "Your seat belt isn't working."

"It works. You just have to push the button down halfway before you push the fastener in. Do that and it will click."

I followed her instructions as beads of sweat formed along my hair line. I think it's easier taking care of Paisley.

When we stopped at a red light, Butterball held up her hand and wiggled it around as if conducting an orchestra, "Magikety, Wickety, Wockety, Spoo!" She did this several times until the light turned green, and then she clapped profusely. "It still works." She snorted with laughter.

"What in the world is she doing?" I asked.

Gabs laughed. "She used to do that with me when I was a little girl. She told me that she knew magic to make red lights turn green. I didn't believe her and told her to prove it." She smiled at the memory. "She proved me wrong every time. If it didn't turn the first time she said the silly lyric, it was because I didn't say it with her, or we didn't say it loud enough, or we weren't saying it at exactly the same time. She is fine, Tess. If this is the worst she gets while medicated, we can handle it."

After a few more magikety-wickety-wockety episodes, we parked in front of Walgreens.

93

"Flash Gordon, right?" I reminded her.

Butterball smiled at me but remained quiet. Gabs hesitated for a second as if she was contemplating something and then dashed inside.

"What a great rollercoaster ride. Let's get cotton candy," Butterball said as she unfastened her seat belt.

"Uh, I'll make you some when we get home." A little white lie never hurt anyone.

"Nope. I want it right in there," she said pointing toward the door that Gabs went through. For someone still on medication, she was still pretty fast. I lunged across the seat in an attempt to catch the back of her shirt as she stepped out of the car.

I should have been able to get out quick, but I couldn't get my seat belt unfastened. Doesn't anyone believe in working seat belts around here? I pushed on the button so hard that it stayed indented. Great, I'm trapped. Butterball stumbled into the store, and I thought of all the chaos she would cause. I tried to slither out of the buckled seat belt, but my hips were too wide. Butterball's purse was on the floor of the back seat. I leaned forward and reached for it, but was caught in a hanging position by the seat belt. I took off my flip flops and reached with my toes for the handle. Three tries later and I had it. With my toes tightly curled around her purse handle, I bent my leg and grabbed it.

Butterball's purse was a black hole. Paperclips, a spatula, and, of all things, she had a huge sweet potato shoved in there. Having a sweet potato in your purse made about as much sense as taking toothpaste on a beach trip...spring trip...whatever it's called. What reason on God's green Earth could she have for keeping a sweet potato in her purse? I tossed it back in, and my fingers touched cold metal. Scissors! I could always count on Butterball. Gabs was going to kill me, but this seat belt was history.

I sprinted into Walgreens. Butterball was nowhere to be seen. I turned down an aisle, slammed into Butterball's back, ricocheted off of her and fell flat on my ass. By the time I came to my senses, she disappeared again.

I found her two aisles over. She faced me but was at the other end of the aisle. She watched as two teenage girls by the personal hygiene aisle pointed at an item on the shelf. One of the girls picked up a black box of condoms and giggled.

The girls were about fifteen years old, by my estimate. One had pink hair, and the other had blue hair. Both wore fishnet stockings, colored bras under sheer blouses, and oversized, embellished cross necklaces. Either they were late for a costume party or were imitating an eighties icon. Yeah, I had two Madonna wannabes right in front of me.

They were so enthralled with the different types of condoms that they didn't hear Butterball as she approached them from behind. She stared at their hair in fascination. To my surprise, she closed her eyes and leaned forward with her tongue.

"Stop," I demanded as she attempted to lick what I knew she believed was cotton candy. All three of them jumped.

"I was just looking," said the panicked, pink-haired girl, and she dropped the box of condoms. "I-I-I have a research paper in health class on safe sex. Yeah."

Sure you do, little girl, and I'm the teacher of your health class. I'll just bring Paisley in. There will be no words necessary.

The blue-haired teen chimed in. "We don't have to explain anything to her. We're old enough to get these." She stood up taller and poked out her chest as if her B cup would be intimidating.

Butterball was licking the air around the pink girl's head. The girl was oblivious to it as she stared at me with her doe eyes.

95

Not worth it. I reached for Butterball's hand, pulled her around the girls and started to walk away.

"That's right. Keep walking," said the blue-haired girl.

I knew I should have kept going. Confrontation isn't a good thing, plus I had Butterball. Where was Gabs when I needed her? She would handle this. They were just little girls. I shouldn't let them get to me. *Just keep your mouth shut, Tess*, I told myself, but it didn't work. I pulled Butterball back and stood just shy of one foot away from them.

"Listen here, Cotton Candy Twins. It's actually embarrassing to get naked with a guy. It looks weird, really weird. But you'll be stupid and do it anyway. I did it, and it ain't all it's cracked up to be, and I had a baby. I left town with that baby, and we are now homeless, penniless, and I'm taking care of...*this* to earn money," I said as I pointed to Butterball who stood there with an opened box of condoms. She blew one up and made a balloon puppet. Butterball saw the pink hair again and moved in.

The pink-haired girl tilted her head to keep it out of reach of Butterball's tongue.

The blue-haired girl looked as if she was considering what I said, but she took a little too long for my comfort. Butterball almost had the pink-haired girl pinned against the condoms and was an inch away from getting her cotton candy.

Maybe a lie will rock their world. "He gave me crabs."

The cotton candy girls jumped. "Eww. I don't want crustaceans in my privates." The blue-haired girl's lips curled up in disgust. She dropped the condoms and left with her hair still intact.

Butterball reached for another box of condoms and sighed. "I miss Simon."

"There you are." Gabs appeared with her arms full of toilet paper and Butterball's prescription in her hand.

I smacked her arm, making her drop the toilet paper. "Flash Gordon, huh?"

***

Butterball crawled into the car and settled on the side I had been in. "Gabba-Gabba, will you tie my shoe?"

Gabs and I looked at her. She was holding both ends of the seat belt I had cut. Gabs looked at me with accusing eyes. I clicked the good seat belt as quietly as possible and sat back.

Ten minutes from home, we approached a construction site. Sweaty men wearing white tank tops and grungy pants worked on the sidewalk on Butterball's side of the car.

Butterball pushed the button to lower the window. "You want some of this? Uh huh, you know you do." Butterball pushed her heavy breasts against the window opening and exposed her cleavage. "I'll bet you've never seen any like these before."

"On my Grandma," yelled one of the construction crew, causing all of the men to laugh. I tugged gently on her shirt, afraid of hurting her. She didn't budge. I couldn't see the window power button as she blocked it from me.

"Gabs, hit the window button. I'll pull her in."

She hit the driver's control button, and the window slid up. Butterball gave her best Gene Simmons impersonation. As the window went up, Butterball's tongue left a trail of spit that streaked the window. She passed out with her face smashed against the glass. The construction crew laughed it off and went back to work.

I think getting my wisdom teeth removed would have been easier than getting Butterball out of the back of the car and into the house. She insisted we all get back in line to go for a rollercoaster ride again. To make matters worse, I accidentally shut the car door on her dress. You could hear it ripping a mile away as a huge piece of her floral-colored dress flapped in the breeze like the red, white, and blue.

We dragged Butterball to the door and turned the knob. It was locked.

"You got her?" Gabs asked.

"What?"

"I have to unlock the house. Hold her for a minute," she said as she dug around in her purse.

Butterball's weight doubled. She turned to face me, and her knees buckled, causing her face to slam into my right breast. If anyone saw us, I'm sure they thought I was breast feeding with all the slobber coming out of her mouth as it saturated my shirt.

"Is it normal for someone to drool this much after surgery? I thought this only happened with dental surgery?" I asked.

"Maybe she was saving it for a special occasion. I don't know! I can't find the keys," Gabs said as she dumped the contents of her purse on the front porch and squatted to sort through the mess.

"Are you serious?" I asked as I shifted Butterball's weight. "Don't you have them on the same keyring as the car?"

"Yes, but I used Butterball's keys, and she took her house key off to make copies for emergencies. She must have forgotten to put it back on. Mine are in the house." She stood up, ran her fingers through her long hair, and assessed the situation. "Okay, I usually keep one of the side windows unlocked. I might be able to shimmy in there with your help. Let's get her on the back porch until we get in the house."

We made Butterball sit in a lounge chair as we stuffed rolled up towels, which we pulled off the railing, around her sides to make her comfortable.

"She looks like a wiener shoved in a hotdog bun," I snorted.

"Butterball, don't move. Just enjoy the view. We will be right back."

Butterball pointed to seagulls flying around on the beach. "You better get my chickens back in the coop."

Gabs grabbed my arm as we rounded the corner of the house. She slid behind an enormous sago palm and stood under the window. When she stood on her toes, her nose came just over the window ledge. She placed her hands on the glass and raised it smoothly.

"Get over here and squat down. I need a stool."

"What?"

Gabs rolled her eyes at me. "I'm in a sun dress, you're in leggings. Get over here."

"Have you ever given a set of keys to Dirk?" I desperately tried to get out of crawling in the sand. "Everyone gives a neighbor a set of keys at some point or other."

"No, I haven't." Irritation was in her voice. "Just get over here. We'll be done before you could ring his doorbell."

I got down on my hands and knees, in the sand, with a sago palm probing my ass through my thin leggings. "Hurry up and get in."

She took one step up on my back in her hard-soled sandals as they dug into my back. "Shoes off, shoes off!" I demanded.

"Sorry," she said as she kicked them to the side and stepped on my back, barefoot. As her heels wedged between my vertebrae, I heard the window slide up.

Whistles came from the direction of the beach. I raised my head and, between the leaves of the sago palm, saw five guys standing on the beach facing us. They hollered some more and whistled. Curiosity made me look up at Gabs, and I was momentarily blinded by her sequined crotch as a breeze blew her sundress up over her shoulders, baring her tanned backside. She slithered through the window, turned around, and hung her head back out.

"You get one freebie, guys. Move on," she yelled.

They applauded her accidental peep show and moved on.

"Head on back to Butterball. I'm going to unlock it, so we can get her in."

We met at the same time at the chair and saw a pile of pillows on the ground. Butterball wasn't there. "Where's Butterball?" she asked.

"Oh, she went to go get butter and bread," I said sarcastically. "I don't know."

Instead of more whistles, we heard giggles. We turned and saw Butterball on the beach, chasing the seagulls and telling them to get back in their coop.

"I swear, if she hasn't already busted her stitches, she will before the day is over," she said as we both ran for Butterball.

Once she was inside, we checked her stitches. All was good. We tucked her in bed as she blamed Diane at the doctor's office for letting the chickens out. We promised her that we would get the chickens back so she would settle down. We retreated to the sanctuary of the living room. Gabs plopped on the couch with her legs splayed, and I sat in a similar pose.

"Please tell me that what Butterball is experiencing is normal for someone still coming out of sedation," I pleaded.

"I really don't know," she answered as she wiped sweat from her brow. "I don't know, but if she asks about Diane when she wakes up, I'm going to tell her I found her and stuck the IV in her car tire."

I laughed. "That should do it. I'm going to get Paisley. Seeing as how I don't have a car, can I borrow yours?" She tossed me her keys, and a few moments later, I was at Dirk's.

Dirk sat on his porch, chewing tobacco in the same position as when I first met him at the car garage. I was able to stay in the car when we dropped off Paisley, but this time I wasn't as lucky.

"I heard your car was stolen," he said, after he spat brown juice out of his mouth.

I shuddered. "Yes, it was."

"You sure you want it back? That girl needs lots of work," he said with one eyebrow raised.

"Yes, I'm sure," I answered. "Was Paisley good for you?" I asked to change the subject.

"Since when is she bad?" I couldn't help but smile at his answer, though I didn't care for him. "Go on in. Kara is in the

100

kitchen." I didn't know his wife's name until then. As a matter of fact, I didn't know his kids' names. I stepped in, and my nostrils were greeted with the smell of homemade bread. Kara hummed a tune as she pulled the fresh bread from the oven. Paisley and Kara's two sons sat on the floor. They tried to teach her patty cake. How come I never tried to do that before?

"Well, hey you," Kara said with a smile as warm as the bread she was placing on a cooling rack.

"Hi," I said and folded my arms protectively across my chest. "I hope Paisley was good for you," I said again to new ears.

Kara glanced sideways at me. "When is she ever bad?" I heard laughter from the front porch and giggling from the floor. Paisley tried to imitate the motions of the boys rolling the dough.

This time I chose to ignore the comment. "I really appreciate you watching her for me. Butterball's surgery went well. She is home, sleeping off the medication."

"Y'all didn't have a problem getting her back home? That's great. I remember Dirk and me taking her to get her wisdom teeth removed about six years ago. There's an entertaining story about that," she said as she laughed out loud at the memory. "But I'll save it for another day. I'm sure you're tired."

My memory was of Butterball's tongue sliding down the window, Cotton Candy girls, Gabs's sequined crotch, and Butterball chasing seagulls on the beach. I wondered if hers was as colorful as mine.

The boys changed games and now played peek-a-boo with Paisley. Twenty tiny fingers covered their eyes, they flung their hands away and said, "Peek-a-boo."

It sent Paisley into fits of giggles. I'd never seen her laugh so much. Paisley took her chunky little fingers and put them on her face, partially covering her eyes. "Oooo," she said as she pulled her fingers away. She laughed at herself. The boys laughed too. Maybe I'd hire them to teach her to walk too.

Paisley Memories | Zelle Andrews

"Colby and Cole have been quite the entertainers today."

Now I knew their names. I scooped Paisley up in my arms, grabbed her baby bag, thanked Kara again, and headed for the door. I waved to Dirk who was still on the porch and fastened Paisley in her car seat.

When I came home, Gabs was still on the couch and had pulled the quilt from the back of the couch to catch a nap. The entire house was quiet. Paisley and I stepped outside and down to the beach. Butterball would have yelled at me for not having sunscreen on her, but I didn't care. I just wanted alone time with her.

She sat in the sand and made sand angels with her fat legs as she moved them from side to side. She made such giant grooves in the sand that she almost toppled over. I picked her up and sat her in my lap as we faced the Gulf. A few of Butterball's "chickens" flew high up in the sky. They dangled on an invisible string as they hovered in place, periodically lifted by a breeze. Small, insignificant waves rolled over and over, occasionally breaking on the beach, leaving broken pieces of seaweed on the shore as they rolled back into the Gulf. The whitish sand glistened with the water and slowly faded to a darker shade, until the next small wave broke on shore. Paisley sat still as if she was taking it all in too.

Two dolphins jumped a few times far out in the water. I thought of all the things that happened to me to get me to this point in my life. Some were choices I'd made; others were out of my hands. Each one changed me a little bit. This very spot was a place where I didn't feel closed in. It was just the sky and water as far as I could see—if I just kept staring in this direction.

The house behind me seemed to get smaller each time I stepped inside, but it was different out here. It was a place to think about my life or just think about nothing, no one to tell me what to do. I could just ponder and sort things out until I came to my own decision. *But, how would I ever know what the right*

102

decision was? How different would my life be without Paisley? As a matter of fact, how different would it be with Paisley? We sat there for a long time, neither of us moving.

A conch shell washed up on shore next to me, and a large crab slowly emerged to look around at its surroundings. It came out in a rush and ran into another larger conch shell a few feet away. It returned, carrying its new home, to the safety of the water. Smart crab. He knew when it had outgrown its home and when to find a larger one. Was that what I did when I left Alabama? Too small and cramped, so I moved on?

I turned Paisley around to face me. She stared at me as if reading my mind. "What are you thinking right now?" I asked. "What do you expect from me? I'm barely an adult. I don't even know how to take care of myself. I lost my car, my Dad, and I think, at times, my sanity. I don't have a job, at least not a real job. I'm mooching off Gabs and Butterball. Maybe you would be better off if I left you here and disappeared."

She still stared at me. "What do you think of that? Would you want Butterball or Gabs as a new mommy? How about Dirk and Kara? You'd have a family to take care of you...an experienced family. I could just ask them to babysit you while I go to the Worm Grunting Festival and not return. I could sell Butterball's camera for a small sum, and then I'd have enough money to catch a bus and just leave. It would be easy. They would keep you, love you, and do right by you." She started to squirm in my arms as her face squinted up. "It's not that I don't love you."

Come to think of it, I had never told her I loved her. I felt it on occasion, or at least I thought I had, but I'd never told her. "I love you," I said as if it would make everything better. "Paisley, just show me a sign that everything will be okay, a burp or a fart; I don't care. Just tell me you want me to raise you and not leave you."

She stared at me for a moment. She put her hands partially over her eyes and said, "Oooo" as she slid them off her face.

103

"I guess that means you love me too." I smiled and hugged her close as she drooled down my back. We sat there for a few minutes and watched seagulls float on invisible strings some more. Paisley reached for the empty conch shell and held it to the side of her head, copying what we had seen Butterball do at the house. Butterball told me that aside from hearing the ocean, you could hear the voices of those you have loved and lost. I'm pretty sure she made up the last part.

"Paisley, let me hold it for a minute." I gently took it from her and held it to my ear. A soothing, whooshing sound filled my ear. Paisley stared at me. I strained to hear Dad's voice, but he didn't answer.

As I lowered the conch shell, I thought I faintly heard the words, "love her" mixed in with the whooshing sound. I raised it quickly to listen again, but the sounds of the Gulf came from the conch. She smiled up at me with the last of the sun's evening rays touching her cheeks. With Paisley on one hip and the conch in my other hand, I headed back to the house.

***

That night we feasted on fish sticks and tater tots. Butterball made my drink bubble out of my nose when she asked us what wine goes with fish. I made sure I had everything together for the Worm Grunting Festival the next day and hit the bed.

CHAPTER TWELVE

Butterball and Gabs were already finished with breakfast when I came out of the bedroom. The aroma of pancakes and sausage made me drool. I was ravenous.

"Can you eat this stuff so soon after surgery?" I asked Butterball.

"Nope, but I can smell it as much as I want," she said and smiled. "I ate scrambled eggs. Dr. Gabrielle told me I need to see how it settles in me before anything else." She rolled her eyes.

"Butterball, you sure you can't just take some codeine and do this yourself?" I was starting to get cold feet.

"You'll do fine," she answered.

I was resigned to the fact I was stuck doing the festival. "By the way, do you remember anything about yesterday after the surgery?"

Butterball pressed her lips together in concentration, "I have a vague memory of eating pink cotton candy and going on a wild rollercoaster ride. Is the fair in town?"

I shook my head.

"Those were pretty good drugs that they gave me, huh?"

"Yep," I agreed.

With all the camera equipment loaded in Gabs's SUV and directions in hand, I kissed Paisley good-bye. "I'll be back," I whispered and gave her a double kiss and a wink.

Halfway to Sopchoppy, panic kicked in again. What was I thinking, taking on this job? I have no professional training except what Butterball showed me. I could break something, lose something, or it could get stolen, like my car. The steering wheel became slick from my sweaty palms. Nightmarish visions of shattered lenses and wormzillas that slithered around and gobbled up all her camera equipment in one big gulp, played through my mind. Soon, I saw cars parked on the side of the road with people coming and going along the side of the street. One car vacated a spot, and I quickly slipped in.

An announcement from a speaker introduced a band called Sopchoppy Mullets. Vendors of all varieties lined the streets. Well, if I took a few photos of everything I saw, there was bound to be something Butterball would use. I clicked away at hand-crafted jewelry, stained glass artwork, and old grannies with millions of crocheted items for sale. You name it, they had crocheted a cover for it. Crocheted wallet covers, crocheted purses, crocheted covers for toasters, crocheted koozies for drinks.

One woman with short, blazing-red hair was giving a demonstration of weaving a rug. Another man, who sported overalls without a shirt, made wind chimes out of beer cans. He cleverly called them "Down South Wind Chimes." I saw one man, with long, wavy, brown hair, selling glass beads. Various sized marbles were displayed in a glass case already covered with dirty fingerprints from customers ogling his art. One of the glass beads made me think of Old Joe's eyeballs at Wakulla Springs. Next to it was the largest marble I'd ever seen. Actually, it was a crystal ball, or at least I would pretend it was. Sure wish I could lay my hands on that one and see what my future had in store for me.

"Hi," I said to the vendor.

"Hi, would you care to look at something?" he offered.

Why not? "Sure. Can I look at the large, clear ball?" I tentatively asked.

"Sure." He unlocked the glass case and reached in with both hands. "It's heavy, so brace yourself."

He placed it in my hands. It was even more gorgeous out of the dirty glass case than it looked when it was in it. Pale, lime green veins, as thin as a thread, appeared to float in the glass ball. I should have asked him what my fortune was. As much as I enjoyed looking at his art, I needed to move on.

"Thank you, but I can't afford it right now," I said.

"No problem. This is my first show, and I'm trying to make a name for myself. Would you like a card? Maybe, in the future, you might be interested in something else?" I graciously took his card and shoved it in my pants pocket.

The local residents who ran for political positions in the county had pictures taken of themselves kissing babies and shaking hands while they passed out flyers under their tents. I sampled fresh-squeezed lemonade from a freckle-faced girl. It hit the spot as the temperature rose.

Cash and items exchanged hands frequently while people walked away and smiled with their newly purchased treasures. The sound of a harmonica and banjo lured me closer to the center of the festival. Several people sat in lawn chairs or lounged on blankets on the grass in front of the stage. One gray-haired couple danced the two-step to the music. I thought I recognized them as the man who chased his wife's hat on the beach.

A little girl with long, wavy, sun-kissed blonde hair sat on a quilt, licking her oversized, rainbow-colored lollipop. Strands of her hair blew forward and stuck to the sticky treasure, but she didn't seem to care. Photo opportunities were everywhere. Butterball would be happy. I clicked away.

A massive rock-climbing exhibition caught my attention. Kids crawled all over it like ants on food at a picnic. One young girl stood patiently as she was strapped into a body harness. Safety ropes were attached too. These were controlled by the vendor so that they could pull the child down if she became scared. She reminded me of the young girl at the water fountain in the mall. Her features favored my Paisley's. Her mother joined her.

"Now, remember, watch the other kids, and do your best. You don't have to make it to the top. Just have fun." Her mother smiled and stepped back, right beside me.

"This is her first time rock climbing. I can't believe I said yes to this," she said, making conversation. "She's wanted to do this for the last three festivals." She gave me a nervous smile and shrugged her shoulders. "I can't say no forever." Her bottom lip quivered.

We watched as the young girl walked up to the rock cliff and sized it up with one upward glance. She didn't look back at her mother for reassurance. We watched as she climbed one rock at a time. I took a deep breath and couldn't believe I was about to broach the subject.

"Does your daughter have Down syndrome?" I asked, half expecting her to slap me for asking such a personal question.

"Yes, she does," she answered, without pausing or giving it a second thought, as if I just asked her to pass the salt at the dinner table.

"If you don't mind me asking you, how old was she when she started to walk?"

"I believe she was around eighteen months old. Her older brothers helped a lot. She wanted to follow them everywhere. The more they tried to get away and do their own thing, the harder she tried," she said and laughed.

Paisley was much older than that. I brushed off the negative thoughts as they crashed in on me and asked if I could take her daughter's photos for the local paper. She agreed immediately. I zoomed in on her daughter's face. She was now eight feet above the ground. You could tell she calculated where to place her foot next. Some kids passed her, and others didn't get three feet off the ground before they became scared and gave up. She made it fifteen feet and decided she didn't want to go any further. She looked down at her spotter below and shook her head. He slowly lowered her down. Her face lit up when her feet hit the ground.

"Did you see me?" she asked her mom as the spotter unharnessed her.

"I did. I'm so proud. Guess what? This lady wants to get your picture for the paper." The young girl said her name was Sadie Fountain, and she smiled so big I giggled to myself. I took a few quick shots, and off they went, arm-in-arm, talking a mile a minute.

I decided right then and there that I was going to strap steel bars on Paisley's legs so she couldn't suck on those toes anymore. I was sure those toes were the source of all my problems in the world, and they were why she wasn't walking yet.

Back at the center of the festival, several children squatted down and rubbed an iron bar back and forth across a wooden stake driven in the ground. It made a horrible grating sound as it sent vibrations into the earth. I watched in amazement as these grayish-brown worms erupted from the soft Sopchoppy soil. All around the children, wiggling worms popped up. The kids were excited. It was as if they struck gold in the California Mountains. At least ten children asked me if I would take their photo with the worms. They thrust their worm-filled hands forward as the worms wiggled to free themselves. I snapped about a dozen photos of worms held by excited boys. Not my thing, but I was sure Butterball would love it.

Many people wore Worm Grunting Festival T-shirts. Eventually, I found my way to the booth selling the shirts. There was an assortment of colors: red, yellow, white, blue, green, pink, and orange. On the front of the shirts, two cartoon worms smiled. They wore top hats and held a banner that said, "Worm Gruntin' Festival." I turned it around and laughed at the back. It said, "I did it all at the Worm Gruntin' Ball."

"Are you taking photos for the paper?" a woman asked.

"Yes, I'm here for Butterball...err, Naomi Mitchell. She had surgery, and I'm helping her out."

She gathered several shirts and put them in a bag. "These are for Butterball. She called and said she forgot to tell you to get her some shirts." She handed me the bag.

"I don't have the money to pay for these," I said as I pushed the bag back.

"It's taken care of, sugar," she said and winked.

I took photos of the reigning horseshoe champion as he demonstrated his skills to newcomers, and I caught the hula hoop contest right at the end.

I listened to the local band, and was polishing off a sample of what might have been fried worms when they announced that last year's Worm Grunting Queen would retain her crown. I had to see this. I worked my way through the crowd and came face-to-face with a little, wrinkled old lady who held a staff in the shape of a gigantic worm. It was the Worm Grunting Queen live and in color.

I wasn't sure if I should bow or not as I'd never met royalty before. I giggled at the absurdity of it.

"You ain't ever seen a Worm Grunting Queen before, have you?" she said.

"No, ma'am, I haven't," I answered, trying to stifle the giggle. "I'm sorry for laughing. It's just...."

She reached out and patted me on the head. "It's okay, dear. It's not as if I woke up one morning after earning my master's degree and said, 'I think I want to become the Worm Grunting Queen when I grow up.'"

I giggled again, and she laughed with me.

"What does one do to deserve such an honor?" I tried to ask with a straight face.

She stood up a little taller. "Well, my grandmother grunted worms for a living, and it provided enough money to feed all eight of her children. One of them was my daddy. I was the wildest of his kids and drove my mother crazy, so she told him

110

to take me to work one day. He grabbed an extra wooden pole and iron bar, and off we went. The first time I tried it, the vibrations made my teeth feel funny," she said as she adjusted her dentures. "It was hard, sweaty work, but when I first saw those brown, little things pop out of the ground, I couldn't believe my eyes. In those days, most everyone fished with worms. I was able to sell them critters, and I bought my mama and daddy a brand new toaster oven." She paused and looked at me. "I know a toaster oven isn't much, but it was a prized possession in our house." Her smile proved it was a sweet memory. "Some of us folks here make a pretty good living of it. I hear that Chappy McMillan made about fifty thousand dollars last year. It helped put his children through college. Not too shabby for a man always digging in the dirt." She smiled. "Anyway, people around here knew my family and heard that we had the fattest worms in the county." She leaned in closer to my ear so I could hear her. "They really weren't the fattest, but we ran with it."

I pulled back and stared at her. "You really take this worm grunting serious, huh?"

She pounded her wooden staff into the ground to emphasize what she was about to say. "They didn't just crown me the Worm Grunting Queen for nothing!" She smiled and patted me on the head again as she disappeared into the crowd of people who congratulated her.

The warm grass became my blanket as I threw a wad of gum in my mouth and listened to the twang of a banjo player on the stage. I was never a fan of the banjo, but it wasn't half bad in the right setting. The members of the Sopchoppy Mullets swayed back and forth to their own music, making their own mullet-style hair swing back and forth.

When they took a break from playing, I packed up Butterball's equipment to head back to the SUV. As I stood up, I tripped on the strap of the camera bag and fell backward into someone's lap.

111

"Oh, my gosh! I am sorry," I stammered and scrambled out of the person's lap, tripped on my own shoelace, and fell again. In a desperate attempt to not land in his lap...again, I turned to catch myself. I ended up with my face smashing into a man's chest.

Two calloused hands cupped my face and tilted my head up. I was two inches away from brown eyes. Brown is a plain color, but not his. The best way to describe them is to envision someone dropping gold glitter in chocolate pudding. Afternoon stubble covered his face, and fresh lemonade was on his breath. I was at a loss for words and just lay there in his arms. A kid slammed two cymbals together close by, and I was brought back to reality.

I jumped back about ten feet and brushed invisible dirt from my clothes out of nervousness. I quickly smoothed my hair down with my fingers and tucked it behind my ears. He rose from his quilt, leaving a little girl sitting there wide-eyed. He stepped closer. I was able to see much more, once I wasn't two inches from his pupils. He was well over six feet tall. His broad shoulders filled out his untucked, white T-shirt. He wore plain, faded jeans with shredded material exposing his knee caps and tan work boots that had seen better days. His light brown hair teased the top of his ears. He stopped about three feet from me.

"Do you need help?" He extended his hands.

I opened my mouth to talk, but instead I inhaled my gum and choked. His smile vanished when I grabbed my throat and gasped for air. He came from behind, did the Heimlich maneuver twice, and my gum shot out like a projectile missile right into the little girl's long, brown hair. I caught my breath as the stranger whirled me around, and a few deep, ragged breathes escaped my throat. He gathered up Butterball's equipment, helped the little girl to her feet, and tossed the quilt over his shoulder.

"Where are you parked?" he asked.

"No, really," I spoke, sounding raspy, as if I worked a sex hotline. "This isn't necessary. I can get to the car myself."

"Nonsense. I already have it in my arms. Just point the way," he said with a crooked grin. Why do guys have to do those sexy, crooked grins that snare girls all the time? *I don't need anyone, I don't need anyone, I don't need anyone.*

"But you are with your family, and she'll miss all the fun," I insisted.

"We were about to leave anyway. I have two strong arms and can carry anything you want." There was that crooked smile again. "You sure I can't help?" he asked.

I looked at him for a long moment. He looked safe. He didn't look the type to attack a woman...especially not one he just saved. Besides, his daughter was with him. And I sure was tired of lugging that camera equipment around.

"I'm less than a quarter of a mile down the road," I said, pointing west.

"Lead the way," he gestured with his one empty hand.

It was strange walking back to the SUV with nothing in my hands. I shoved them in my pockets and listened to both of them as they fell in step behind me.

"Daddy, who is that lady?" the little girl asked.

"I don't know, Penny. Just a lady who needs some help."

"You saved her life. She spat gum in my hair, and she didn't even tell you her name. That's not very nice," I heard her whisper loudly to her daddy. "Daddy, how are you going to get this gum out of my hair?"

"We'll figure it out later," he answered.

When I arrived at the car, I unlocked the trunk, and he loaded the equipment for me.

"Thank you for helping me. I'm sorry about your daughter's hair." I looked down at her holding her dad's hand as my wad of gum clung to her beautiful, long, brown hair at chin level. I was nervous and said the first thing that popped into my head. "There should be a warning label on the side of gum

113

packages 'Warning, gum may be hazardous to your hair.'" I smiled.

"You should write the surgeon general of gum," he said with a crooked grin again.

"Who? Oh, yeah."

"Well, I'll see you around," he said as he turned to leave with his daughter. She turned around, stuck her tongue out at me, and crossed her eyes. The death curse for kids of her age. I barely heard her tell her dad that they still didn't know my name.

"Tess!"

He turned around. "What?"

"My name is Tess." His little girl rolled her eyes. "Tess Cooper."

"See you around, Tess Cooper," he said.

CHAPTER THIRTEEN

On the way home, I took a detour, to clear my head, and ended up in Crawfordville. I stopped at Myra Jean's to grab a soda. When I pulled out a couple of dollars to pay, a small, oblong piece of paper fell from my wallet. It was wadded up and about the length and width of my finger. It took a second to remember it was the adoption agency number I'd kept from my visit to Wakulla Springs. I picked it up and held it for a moment.

"You want me to throw away that straw wrapper?" asked the cashier.

I could hand this to her, watch it get tossed in the trash with leftover food from the tables and used napkins, or I could keep it—keep it until I was sure of what I wanted to do. That little piece of paper would give me an out, a way to be me again. The cashier was patiently waiting with her hand held out for me to decide. I slipped it in my pocket and smiled.

In the time it took me to walk from Myra Jean's to the car, I knew what I had to do. I ended up at a gas station pay phone and called the number on my crumbled up paper. My hands shook so badly that I entered the wrong number the first time, wasted the quarter, and entered the number again.

"Hope Adoption Agency. May I help you?"

I opened my mouth to speak, but no words came out.

"Hello?"

"Yes," I forced the words out. "I need your address."

"2-2-1-4 Cuttergrass Lane."

No one at home would miss me yet. The Worm Grunting Festival started early that morning, and it was barely noon. I could be there and back before evening. The festival wasn't supposed to end until five p.m. anyway. I could make up a story that kept me busy, even after the festival was over, if necessary. I bought a map of Thomasville, Georgia, and made it there in less than two hours. It wasn't what I expected. It had once been a residential area. Old houses, now converted into stores and offices, lined the street. The adoption house was situated right between Shirley's Hair Salon and Gordon and Sheri's Antiques. Across from them was a playground for kids. I wondered if the staff at the adoption agency ever gave out flyers to mommies at the park. Probably not.

Dampness began to saturate my armpits. I walked up the concrete steps, crossed the oak plank porch, and stood in front of the door. Do I ring the doorbell or just walk in? This was a place of business, but it was also a house. I stepped back to make sure the house numbers were correct. They were. I stepped up on the porch, took a deep breath, and rang the doorbell. My left hand twitched, and I shoved it in my pocket just as the door opened. A middle-aged woman greeted me with a smile.

"Hello. How may I help you?"

What do I say? I have a baby and I want money. You want money, and I have a baby. Let's make a deal? "I want to learn more about the adoption process."

She stepped back and held the door open. "Come on in and have a seat. Someone will be right with you."

The living room was set up office-style, with two couches for customers and a large, metal desk with a computer and file cabinet behind it. She walked to a back room and returned quickly, taking her seat behind the desk.

I could feel the dampness under my arms begin to spread across my back. "Do you have a restroom?"

116

She smiled again and pointed to her left. I entered the restroom and shoved toilet paper under my armpits to soak up the sweat. A small hand dryer was installed on the wall. I locked the door, stripped my shirt off and held it under the dryer to dry each pit section. Here I was in Thomasville, Georgia, in an adoption agency bathroom, half naked, with toilet paper under my pits. Life was grand.

Redressed and refocused I sat down on a chair in the living room. *Magazines. They must have magazines here,* I thought. I thumbed through the magazines on the coffee table in front of me. Everything involved adopting and parenting. A large, white binder was full of pictures of mothers and fathers holding babies, toddlers, and older kids. The children didn't resemble the parents at all. It was a photo album compiled of adoptees and their new parents. I pulled it closer and rested it on my lap.

A young, married couple exited the back room, followed by an elderly woman who told them she would be in touch. I quietly closed the binder. The young couple couldn't have been older than their mid-twenties. They both looked excited. When they saw me sitting on the couch, they immediately looked at my belly as if I was a prospective mother-to-be. The woman gently encouraged their exit and approached me. She sat down on the couch beside me, and her black pencil skirt rose just above her knee.

"It is my understanding that you are interested in learning more about the adoption process with our agency."

The white vinyl book was stuck to my legs and caused them to sweat. The book made a sucking sound as I peeled it off my lap. "Yes."

"Well, follow me, and you can ask all the questions you want." As I stepped into her office, the door closed with a loud slam, and I jumped.

"Have a seat." She walked behind her desk and sat in her chair as I sat in a tan, upholstered, high-back chair. "Sorry about the door. I've been meaning to get it repaired. It has a mind of

117

its own." She smiled. "So," she said and leaned forward with her hands on her desk and eyes focused on me, "Are you wishing to adopt?"

"No. Good grief, no," I stammered.

Her shoulders relaxed, and her eyes refocused on my abdomen. "Are you pregnant and wanting to give your baby another home?"

"No to the first and yes to the second."

"Okay, we are getting somewhere here," she said and walked around the desk. She leaned her rear on the front of it to reduce the distance between us. "Share with me the situation you are in."

What do I say? I'm selfish, and I don't want to be responsible for a child who has needs greater than mine? I took a deep breath. "I have a baby."

She smiled and patiently waited for me to continue as a wave of nausea began to build up, and my armpits became wet again. "I have a baby. A baby girl with special needs." My eyes trailed off out the window as I expected her to say she couldn't help me.

"She has Down syndrome." I got ready to be escorted out, knowing they wouldn't be able to help me.

"Are there other medical conditions?"

"She hasn't started to walk yet. Well, she can stand and walks if she has something to hold onto. She isn't talking yet either. She babbles, but nothing I can understand. Look, if you can't help me, just tell me now, so I don't waste your time."

"Relax. We have adoptee families that will love a child regardless of a disability." She walked to her desk, sat in her black-leather office chair, and tinkered around on her computer for a minute. When she turned the monitor around for me to view, my heart skipped a beat.

"These are prospective couples and a few single moms who are interested in adopting a baby. I have a file on each one."

118

One couple had their arms wrapped around each other. She was a petite blonde, and he was very muscular with short, black hair. They looked about the age my dad was before he died. Their clothes looked expensive. A diamond the size of my front tooth was on her left hand. They oozed of money. The woman slowly scrolled down the page for me to view more. On the fourth page, there was another couple. He wore a police uniform and was tall and lean with a bald head. The wife was short and plump and reminded me of the classic elementary-school teacher. One woman was all by herself in a picture and stood in front of a barn. Maybe Paisley would like to live on a farm. Her light, brown hair was braided to the side, and she wore a white, flowing sundress with brown cowboy boots. Why would anyone who was single want to take on the responsibility of caring for a baby, much less one with a disability? So many families eager to take my baby. My chest tightened again.

She clicked on another icon on the lower screen, and an entirely new window opened. "These families have advised us that they have no restriction on a baby, regardless of race, gender, age, or disability. This means that your daughter might be perfect for one of these families." I scanned the pages, and it was more of the same, everyone smiling the brightest smile possible, wearing their best clothes, to give the best impression. One couple looked too perfect. The husband stood behind the wife as she sat in a chair. He wore a suit, the type you would wear to the office, and every button was buttoned on the jacket. His hair was slicked back. One of his hands was on the back of the chair, and the other was on his wife's shoulder. She sat so straight you would have thought she had a steel rod through her back in place of her spine. Her smile was spread wide enough that it caused the veins in her neck to bulge out. Her clothes were vintage and out of the 1950s—pearl necklace, low pumps, and the classic, solid-colored 1950s dress. Would they raise Paisley as if it was the 1950s? No, not them. Please not them. The last two couples pictured were more my style of parents. I could see either one of them raising Paisley. Both couples were young and wore jeans with button-down shirts. Relaxed smiles spread across their faces instead of tense, fake ones. One couple showed the entire family. Their children were of different races than the parents. Everyone looked happy. No judging, no prejudices against someone…different.

I flipped back to the couple in blue jeans.

"What are their names?" I asked.

"Dylan and Maggie FitzGerald. They have wanted a child for a few years. Wonderful couple. They have agreed to an open adoption."

"You mean I could see my daughter even after I've given her up?"

"Each open adoption is different. A few adoptive parents share everything. Others are more particular. It would depend on what the family wants to share with you. They may just allow periodic, scheduled phone calls during the holidays and an email address in order to correspond, or they may even give you their address and phone number to arrange personal visits with the child and you. You can choose your family, even meet them, but you will not have a say in raising the child.

"We also offer closed adoptions. This is where you relinquish all your rights, and we choose the family. You would not have a choice, and you would not be able to learn who her new parents are as the records would be sealed. We have been leaning more toward the semi-private adoptions as statistics show it is better for the child, as well as both sets of parents. In your case, parent.

"I want you to know that we consider ourselves to be the birth mother's advocate as well as the adoptive parents'."

I looked out the window at a bird perched on a branch. I wasn't sure what to say.

"I know this is a lot to take in," she said as she rose. "How old are you, dear? Does your family know you are here?"

"I don't have a family anymore. Mom died when I was born. Dad died of cancer several months ago. No one but me and Paisley."

"What a beautiful name."

"Will they change her name?" Not that it mattered. She was named after a blanket and a nurse, for Pete's sake.

"That would be entirely up to the couple. I know that this is an emotional time for you and very stressful."

More questions came to me. "Do these families live locally? If I don't trust myself to pick the right family, will you do it? I mean you, personally?"

"Again, we aren't able to tell you much about the family without their consent. But, yes, I will choose the family personally if you wish for me to. Are you sure about this?"

"Yes, I would want you to choose the family."

"No, I mean are you sure about giving your baby up for adoption?" She reached out to touch my hand, and it was warm as it covered mine. "We can refer you to a counseling center if you feel you would benefit from it. Sometimes talking to someone can help you come to a decision you are happy with. You are young. I can see how you might feel unprepared to raise a baby on your own, especially one with special needs. But you need to be honest with yourself as to why you wish to give her up."

Her hands were warm. If she wrapped her arms around me would they be as warm? Like a blanket? I needed a warm blanket right now. "I've been thinking of finding her a new home for a while. I don't have a car for transportation. The one I came here in is borrowed. I don't have a steady job, and I have no family to help me." My breath came out ragged. "I once left a baby doll at a park because she got her hair tangled in the park swing. I can't keep her."

Despite how pitiful I sounded, the woman smiled and giggled a little. She squeezed my hand. "I once tied my little brother to the tree in our backyard when I was a teenager and told him that the tree was alive and would eat him if he cried or told on me."

I stared at her in shock. She patted my hand and stood up.

"We all did silly things in our youth. I have three children of my own and love them to bits. I would never consider doing something to them. We all grow up, young lady. And if you have taken care of this young child with no help from others all this time, and she is still breathing, well, dear, that is no small feat. Kudos to you."

I wished she was my mother. Had my mother been as kind and nurturing as she was? I hoped so. Is this what it would have been like for me if my mother had lived? I think I missed out on something. How could you miss someone you'd never met?

"No, I'm sure about this. I think a closed adoption would be best," I said.

"We can draft up a general agreement. It isn't binding until the final stage of the adoption."

We spent the next hour going over the general agreement, the amount of money I would receive, and how soon she might be back in touch with me. I hesitated to give her Butterball's phone number. She explained that this was just the beginning. That she was getting the ball rolling, so to speak. There would be much...much more paperwork to follow and a medical exam for Paisley.

"I am staying with a friend, and it would upset her to know what I am doing. Can I just call you maybe once or twice a week to check on the status? I have no other way to do this."

"This is a little unorthodox from my normal practice, but I am willing to work with you."

"I promise to check back twice a week. Thank you." We shook hands, as casually as if I had just sold a car, she escorted me to the door, and then I left.

I cried all the way back to Butterball's and pulled over once to throw up. If this was the right decision, then why was I feeling so sick?

CHAPTER FOURTEEN

The air conditioning in Gabs's house felt refreshing. I made myself a glass of sweet tea and walked to the window to get a view of the water. Gabs and Paisley were making a sand castle on the beach. Well, it was Gabs doing the architecture work and Paisley acting as a one-woman demolition team.

I walked out, sat down in the sand next to them, and sipped my tea. Paisley crawled over and made a moat in front of the castle when she knocked the tea out of my hand. Just Paisley being Paisley. I sighed and let her settle in my lap.

"Did you get good pictures?" Gabs asked, as she cupped a handful of wet, dripping sand from the castle's moat and drizzled designs on the castle walls.

"I took so many pictures that I have a blister on my pointer finger."

"She'll be glad. Did you have a good time?"

I thought of the Sopchoppy Mullets, the rock climber, the Worm Grunting Queen, and the man with golden flakes swimming in his brown eyes. "Let's say…, it was interesting."

"Ah," Gabs said as she looked up. "Something happened. I can tell by the look on your face."

"I met someone," I said.

She stopped what she was doing and stared at me.

123

"And?" she pushed for me to continue.

"There is no *and*. I just met someone. I was choking, and he did the Heimlich and saved me."

"I told you not to sample the fried worm appetizers," Gabs teased. "Are you okay? What were you choking on?"

"Gum," I answered.

She stared at me in disbelief. "Little kids chewing gum."

"Well, it ended up in a little kid's hair."

She laughed. "I'll bet that went over great with the parents." She smiled, but it vanished when she looked back at the house. "I guess I better head back into the dungeon and cook supper for Butterball. She's been awful today. She thought you had stolen all the equipment, hocked it, and left us here with Paisley because you were gone so long. She said she would hunt your ass down and use you as feed for her chickens."

I didn't smile at the first part, because it was too close to the truth of what I considered last night. I laughed nervously as we headed inside.

She took the shirts to Butterball's room and showed them to her. She insisted on wearing the oversized pink one although it clashed with her hair. Butterball went on the back porch and watched the sun go down as she fell asleep in the lounge chair. I flipped through the channels and let Paisley watch cartoons for a few minutes.

"Gabs, can you watch her for a sec? I have to use the bathroom." She nodded, and I left Paisley on the floor. I had barely sat down on the toilet when chubby little fingers slid under the door in search of me. I hadn't closed the door all the way, and she was able to push it open. A few minutes later, Butterball appeared in the bathroom doorway while I was holding Paisley in my lap, singing patty cake.

"And y'all think I'm strange on medication. At least I ain't sitting on a toilet, singing nursery rhymes."

***

We feasted on spaghetti that night. Butterball slurped up the noodles in chicken broth as she was afraid to eat the spicy sauce. Paisley feasted on her toes for dessert which she did almost every night. Once Paisley had her bath and was settled in her crib, I crawled into bed with a book I pulled off the shelf. Based on the cover, it was the classic "happily ever after" type of book. I fell asleep by page thirty-three, wishing I could have my own "happily ever after."

***

Two hours later, I ran into Gabs coming out of the guest bathroom as I was going in.

"We are back to square one. The noodles and broth aren't settling in good for Butterball. She took over my bedroom and bathroom, so she doesn't have to share a bathroom with anyone," said Gabs.

"How bad is it?"

"Let's just say that now wouldn't be a good time for the plumbing to act up."

I grimaced. We both heard Butterball's feet hit the floor as she ran to the bathroom, cussing.

Gabs stared at my bed head for a minute. "Tomorrow, you and Paisley are getting haircuts. My treat." I didn't argue. All I wanted to do was pee and get back in bed. I agreed.

The next morning Gabs dropped us off at the hair stylists. "Ask for Loretta. She'll treat you right. Tell her you're staying with us. I'll be back in a couple of hours."

When I walked in with Paisley on my hip, I saw the same little girl with long, brown hair from the festival, the one I spat my gum on. Her waist-length hair lay on the black and white checkered linoleum floor. She sported a new, page boy cut. She frowned at me. I turned crimson with shame.

"Good morning, Tess."

125

My worm-grunting hero was sitting next to an old man reading a hunting magazine.

"Her hair," I said flabbergasted. "You couldn't get the gum out?"

He walked over to me to finish the discussion. "By the time we got home, she'd fiddled with it so much there was nothing I could do."

"No, I didn't," exclaimed Penny as she pouted in embarrassment.

"I tried to cut it myself, last night, but made it worse."

"I feel horrible. Is there anything I can do?" I thought for a moment. "Let me pay for the haircut." It would mean I wouldn't get mine done, but that was the least I could do.

Paisley reached out to him, something she had never done with a man. I stepped back and turned a little, keeping her out of reach.

Before we could finish the conversation, the barber called him over. I spied from over the top of my magazine, watching, as his hair was cut. I became irritated when I thought they cut it too short. Why should I care? I don't know this guy. Paisley took turns ripping pages out of magazines and sucking on her toes. It was a complete embarrassment.

His daughter came and sat down beside us. "I'm seven years old, you know. Practically a woman," she said proudly. She picked up a woman's magazine and saw her dad as he looked at her sternly. She slowly placed the woman's magazine down and made it look as if she changed her mind and chose a children's magazine instead. She was smooth, this one.

"I think this haircut makes me look older. What do you think?"

"Oh, yes, at least eight and a half."

She held the magazine higher in front of her face, using it as camouflage. She whispered to me in a most serious tone. "Well, don't get any ideas about my daddy. He may be divorced, but I keep him very busy taking care of me. He doesn't have time for anyone else," she insisted.

"I understand. I'm very busy too, taking care of Paisley," I shifted her on my lap, and Penny stared at her face.

"Her eyes look funny," she said.

I stiffened, trying to think of how to respond. Before I could think of anything, she spoke again. "Oh, well, my hair looks funny," she said, as though it was equally comparable. Penny started showing Paisley pictures in her magazine, and Paisley kept grabbing the pages. Each time she did this, Penny took Paisley's hands away, and said, "Look, no touch."

After several tries, I noticed that Paisley reached part way and slapped her own hands on her legs. Penny smiled and told her she was being so good. My hero paid for his and Penny's haircuts before I could stop him.

"Who's next?" yelled a female.

"I'm waiting on Loretta," I answered.

"That's me," said a short woman whirling scissors on her fingers like a baton.

I sat in the chair and discussed how I wanted my hair cut, and Paisley climbed all over me, trying to get back to Penny.

"You are going to have to ask someone to hold her, so I can wash and cut your hair, or we will have to reschedule," she said.

"I'll do it," said my worm-grunting hero. "By the way, my name is Aaron. Aaron McMasters. He reached to take Paisley before I could answer and went to sit with Penny. They entertained Paisley the entire forty minutes it took to wash, cut, and style my hair. When I turned to look at the new haircut, my jaw dropped. I didn't realize how bad my hair looked, until I saw it polished and groomed to perfection. Loretta was *good*.

"My daughter needs a haircut too, but I don't think she will sit still."

"I have forty years of experience with children, honey," she said. "Bring that little jar of strawberry jam over here." I looked

127

on her counter and saw a small baby jar filled with red gooey jam. Aaron handed Paisley to me.

"You just hold your daughter." She smeared the jelly on Paisley's fingers. Paisley slowly brought her fingers to her mouth and sucked on them one by one. Great, now she would be a finger-sucking freak too—not just her toes. But with this distraction, Loretta had Paisley's hair snipped short in no time.

Loretta wiped the residue of jelly from Paisley's fingers as I paid the cashier. Aaron and Penny chatted with another barber. I walked over to thank him for watching Paisley.

"You're welcome. I see you aren't chewing gum today," he teased.

"Yeah. I'm trying to cut back. I have a gum patch on my arm." We both smiled, and Penny looked confused.

For an awkward moment, we just stood there smiling at each other until I heard a horn honk. Gabs was in the parking lot, waiting. I excused myself, and we loaded up in the SUV.

"I saw you talking to a cute guy. Was he your worm guy?" she asked.

Worm guy. That sounded weird, but I guess worm-grunting hero is no better. At least now, I knew his name. "Actually, his name is Aaron McMasters."

She nodded. "I've heard of him. I think he works in carpentry or something construction-ish."

"Construction-ish? We must contact *Wikipedia*, so they can add your new word," I teased.

"I have a lot more words for them to add since taking care of Butterball. That pain medication makes her say things I've never heard her say before. She is awful."

"Tell me what you know of Aaron?" Curiosity had gotten the best of me.

"Not much, just the basics. He has been divorced for five years. His wife—I can't recall her name—left him for the lawn-maintenance guy. I think she has been in town twice since they divorced, and it was for money, not Penny. Butterball could tell you more. Aaron occasionally brings Butterball venison from his hunting trips. She has taken lots of photos of his daughter."

She cut her eyes sideways at me and slapped my thigh. "Are you interested?"

"What? Oh, no. No. I was just…curious," I stammered as I adjusted my seat belt that was suddenly too tight.

"Uh huh," she said. "Well, I think he's a good-looking guy. You could do worse." She glimpsed at Paisley. "As a matter of fact, you did that already with Thom. The only thing good that came from that relationship was her." She smiled at Paisley.

She really thinks that *she* is something good? I've been waiting for something good to happen in my life for the past three years. Had it already happened, and I was oblivious to it?

"I can arrange a double date if you want me to. Me and the professor, you and Aaron."

"Absolutely not. I said I wasn't interested. Don't you think I have enough on my plate? I don't need a man in my life right now messing things up."

"Oh, of course not, because you are doing such a fine job of it all by yourself," she shot back. "I didn't say you needed a man. Just that having one around can be nice once in a while." Her voice softened. "Even if it is only for friendship and to occasionally fix the plumbing or change a tire."

"I don't need a plumber. I can unclog drains just fine, and in case you have forgotten, my car was stolen. No tires need to be replaced. I see no reason for a man here."

"Yeah, Butterball told me about Simon's ring," she said, flowing easily into my change of subject. "Simon was the perfect man for her. I keep telling her that one day she'll be in love again, but she is focused on her photography." She frowned. "I guess if that makes her happy, who am I to judge?"

Her expression changed. "So, back to construction man."

I slammed my head in the back of the headrest. "Can you just please let this go?"

A seductive smile set on her face. "Did you wear your thong?"

"Gabrielle!" Her boldness surprised me. She laughed, turned up the radio and sang off-key the rest of the way home. I had two choices, tell her to stop singing and risk the conversation getting back to Aaron or listen to her singing until it became tinnitus. I chose to listen to her singing blissfully off-key. Genetics run strong in her family.

Butterball ventured from the bedroom and made herself comfortable on the couch with the aid of pillows tucked behind her back and sides. She was master of the remote control and settled on a classic movie on television.

"Look at you. You are out of the room," Gabs said, hoping to get her bedroom back.

"Don't get too excited," Butterball said deflated. "This is a trial run to see if I can make it to the hall bathroom in time. Just don't get between me and Johnny."

"Which bathroom can we use?" I asked.

"The one I ain't in."

After raiding the refrigerator of leftovers and watching Butterball eat chicken soup, we waited for the gauntlet run. Ten minutes later, I went to the kitchen and began to clean. Paisley crawled after me and pulled open the bottom cabinet. She squealed with excitement as she pulled the small aluminum lids out and began to clap them together.

Eventually, the inevitable happened, and her toes ended up in her mouth. I yanked them out abruptly, she lost her balance, fell backward, and banged her head on the tile floor with a resounding crack. She screamed in pain as I picked her up, feeling guilty.

"What happened? Did you pinch her again?" accused Butterball.

"No, I didn't pinch her again. I mean no, I didn't pinch her, period. She just fell backward, that's all." I picked her up and ran my hands over her head. No gushing blood or goose egg.

The four of us settled on the couch to watch movies for the rest of the night. At the climax of the first one, Butterball shot off the couch with a panicked look on her face. She looked toward Gabs's doorway, which was about thirty feet away from where she stood. She quickly turned her head toward the hallway, which was about twenty feet away. She bolted for the hallway bathroom and slammed the door, shaking the collectibles on the shelves.

"Turn it up, so I don't miss anything," she yelled.

"We can pause it."

"I think I'm going to homestead this bathroom," she said through the door and courtesy flushed. "Just turn it up."

Between flushes, she yelled at us. "What did they say?"

We watched the remaining few minutes of the movie while Butterball was in the bathroom.

"I guess she's in my room again. I'm turning in. 'Night." Gabs kissed Paisley on the forehead and headed toward Butterball's old bedroom.

"Whoever's coming my way, I need more toilet paper."

Gabs pulled a roll from the hall closet, cracked the bathroom door open and threw it in.

"Thanks. You're a keeper," said Butterball, and she flushed twice.

I retreated with Paisley. While clearing pictures off my bed, I ran across one of Paisley I had taken on the beach. I wrote my name, her name, and our ages on the back, and quickly put it in an envelope to mail to Hope Adoption Agency, so they would have a picture of Paisley to show the parents. I had my first night with no nightmares or any dreams that I could recall.

***

We all considered buying stock in toilet paper, but Butterball recovered quickly after the weekend. Two weeks later, she was in her own room. Gabs was elated to have her

131

room back and fumigated it in the process. She found almost a dozen dirty glasses under the bed and an old pizza box but didn't complain. She was just happy to have her room back.

CHAPTER FIFTEEN

Butterball and Gabs decided to take Paisley to Tallahassee for the afternoon. The entire house was empty and I had it all to myself. I had never been alone in the house before. The silence was odd. Nobody stirring around in the kitchen, cooking supper. Nobody complaining. I thought I would enjoy this, as this was what I'd wanted all along, or so I thought. The sun streamed in through the windows facing the Gulf, inviting me outside. When I reached the French doors to go outside, the phone rang.

"Hello?"

"Tess Cooper, please," said an unfamiliar voice.

"This is she."

"Ah, Miss Copper, this is Alice from Hope Adoption Agency."

My feet went numb. I fumbled for the counter to steady myself. How did they get this number? I specifically said I would call them. How much time had passed since my visit there? I'd lost track of time.

"We received your picture of Paisley, and I have wonderful news. We have a couple who is interested in adopting your daughter. They are in their thirties. They would prefer a semi-adoption, but I can tell you a little bit about them as they gave permission. He has a well-established law practice, and she is a special-education school teacher. They are eager to adopt."

She paused giving me time to register everything.

"They saw the photo that you mailed to us and instantly fell in love with Paisley. They think the name is adorable. I don't have favorites regarding placement of children, but I can tell you this, if I was in your shoes, this is the family I would want my child to go to."

I'll bet she says that to all the mothers about to sever the umbilical cord.

"Okay. I'm listening," I said, hoping she would take the hint that I needed to know more.

She cleared her throat. "Well, you know the typical cost of adoption as we covered that during our meeting. It would normally be twenty-five-thousand dollars, but they are willing to double the amount if they can take Paisley home by next weekend. The child would have to go into foster care temporarily while health checks are conducted. I am willing to work late every day to complete all the necessary paperwork. You would need to come to Thomasville to sign paperwork as well, of course. But it is doable."

Doable. Giving up Paisley is doable. I would be selling my baby for fifty-thousand dollars. I don't know of any used cars at that price...

"Miss Cooper?"

"Yes?"

"When you were here last, you talked about all that you would not be able to give to her at this point in your life. This family can give her that and more. I know you want what is best for Paisley: a stable environment, routine, someone who can take care of medical expenses, should they arise, for a child who has disabilities. You also mentioned what you wanted to do with your life. This money would help you go to college if that is something you still want. Start a new life, help you get roots put down so that when you become a mother again, you will be ready."

She was saying all the right things. I couldn't disagree.

"Ma'am, I need time to think about this."

"How much time?" her voice waivered.

"How much time do I have?"

"Well, how about I call you back in two days. Will that work for you?"

"Two days. Yes."

My feet were still numb. I needed Butterball and Gabs. I needed to know what they thought. Wait, no I didn't. This was my decision. It didn't affect them, just Paisley and me. I needed fresh air.

Fresh, salty air brushed my face when I opened the glass, French doors. The sun warmed my cheeks. Waves gently rolled in and back out as if beckoning me to go for a swim. Wakulla Springs was the only time I'd been in the water. As much as I'd always wanted to see the Gulf, that was all I'd done, just seen it. I was ready to experience it. My heart raced as I ran into the water, fully clothed. A warm wave splashed on my thighs. My toes sank in the sand, and then it loosened around them as the wave receded, causing me to lose my balance, falling face first into the water. I laughed out loud at myself as salt water stung my eyes. I took five, gigantic steps and dove under. The warm water rushed past my face, invigorating me. I swam underwater until I was almost out of breath. When I emerged, I was chest deep on a sand bar. The waves gently lifted me off the sand bar and brought me back down.

This was the most free I'd felt since I'd been here. I closed my eyes and faced the sun to feel its warmth on my skin. The yellow glow that seeped through my eyelids was eclipsed, followed by a splash. My eyes shot open as I stepped back. Two dolphins appeared within ten feet of me. With my jaw hung open in surprise, I watched as the dolphins played and jumped around me. My initial fear became awe. They slowly moved in closer. I reached out just as one of the dolphins' noses surfaced two feet away. It was a baby! It couldn't have been more than two or three feet long. It stared at me with black, curious eyes. My hand shivered with excitement. The baby inched closer until

135

my fingertips hovered above its nose. I touched it. *Oh, my gosh. I touched it.*

One of its eyes differed from the other. The eyelid was almost sealed closed. I looked closer, thinking it might be an injury. There was no scar. The dolphin must have been born with a deformed eye. The baby dipped underwater as the mother circled me. She jumped a few times, and her baby followed suit. She watched me with those same black, curious eyes. Would this one be as trusting? I slowly stretched my hand forward and boldly stroked her nose and the side of her face. Her baby ventured too far, and she broke away quickly to round her baby up.

The three of us swam in the shallows together, both of them coming in frequently to watch me. Curiosity of the other was shared by all of us. A crowd gathered on the beach to watch. The temptation was too much for some kids as they tried to join in, but as soon as they entered the water, the dolphins dove under. I splashed around trying to get them back to the surface. I wasn't done yet. A wall of light gray rose before my face, just inches away, as the mother jumped over me and splashed behind me, taking my breath away in awe of her grace. Cheers came from the beach as the dolphins disappeared beneath the water.

I stood there for a while, hoping they would return. The kids that entered the water gave up and returned to the shore and soon departed. I sat on the empty beach, waiting for the dolphins to return, but they were gone.

Beside me stood a partially collapsed sandcastle. It reminded me of the old, ruined castles I'd seen in picture books as a child—the type you find in the countryside of Europe where the walls have crumbled due to war and age. A large footprint had smashed the top of this sandcastle. Broken shells shoved in the sides made cracks in the sand walls. I felt I must repair this broken home and make it whole again. I rebuilt it and carefully removed the broken shells, repaired the castle roof, caulked the cracks in the walls with wet sand and smoothed them until no trace of the previous damage showed. The discarded shells spelled out "Paisley" in front of the castle.

Proud of myself, I stood back and smiled at my creation. It was all starting to make sense now. This was Paisley's castle, not the sandcastle, but the house behind it. She did have a family. She did have a home, and so did I…, if they would have us.

***

Salty water dripped from my clothes onto the floor of Gabs's house as I dialed the number. And I dialed it right the first try. The phone rang four times before Alice answered.

"Hope Adoption Agency. Alice Spears speaking."

"Miss Spears, this is Tess Cooper."

"Ah, yes, I thought you wanted two days?"

"It's not necessary. I have made my decision."

"Wonderful! I will call the family today and schedule a time for them to come in to sign the paperwork. You are doing a wonderful thing, Miss Cooper," she praised.

I took a deep breath. "Yes, I am, because I am keeping Paisley. Tell the family that I'm sure they will find another baby to love, but Paisley is for me to love, and only me." I hung up because there was nothing more to say. I stood there expecting her to call me back, but the phone didn't ring. I'd never sounded so sure of myself. Was that really me talking on the phone? The decision was made. I was keeping Paisley. Had I messed up a perfect opportunity for Paisley to have a mother *and* a father? I thought I was doing the right thing.

I peeled out of my freezing clothes before jumping in a hot shower and then quickly towel-dried my hair. The clock read three p.m. I had been in the water for a few hours and didn't even realize it.

Gabrielle, Butterball, and Paisley came in the house as I was getting dressed. Smiles covered their faces, even Paisley's.

"We had a great time," Gabs said. "How was your day? Let me guess. You lounged around in your underwear and took a long nap."

I smiled to myself. "Something like that."

CHAPTER SIXTEEN

Within one month, Butterball was making the occasional trip to the grocery store. Three months later, she resumed her photography jobs. My car was still missing, and I needed money to buy a new one, so I offered to stay indefinitely, to help on any photography jobs that were available. My pictures of the Worm Grunting Festival made it in the *Wakulla News*, and with Butterball telling people of my talent, I soon had my own clientele. It started with a kid's birthday party and then an anniversary. I was stashing away every penny I could for a car.

I saw Aaron around town with his daughter. Her hair stayed short, so she must have liked it. We always exchanged hellos but never anything more. It was best this way. His daughter would steer him the other way if she saw me before he did, making it obvious he wasn't available. It didn't matter, as I wasn't available either. Paisley was no closer to walking than I was to finding my car. I was in a never-ending cycle of earning money, but never enough.

Dirk and his family invited us to their house for Thanksgiving. The boys had grown big in a matter of months, and Paisley continued to learn new games with them but refused to walk when they tried to encourage her. When we sat around the table, Dirk had each of us say what we were thankful for.

"I'm thankful for good surgeons, great neighbors, and unexpected company," said Butterball as she smiled at me.

"I'm thankful for a friend coming back in my life and good plumbing," Gabs said and giggled.

Dirk spoke for him and his wife. "We are thankful for our friends and our health."

His sons both giggled and said in unison as if they practiced it, "We are thankful for desserts."

Colby leaned over to me and whispered, "Mom has banana pudding in the refrigerator."

It was my turn. What was I thankful for? My car had been stolen, Paisley still wasn't walking yet, and there was a little girl in town spreading the word that I was a bubble gum warrior, and it wasn't safe to leave your house without a shower cap when out in town in case they ran into me. I looked around at their anticipating faces. Who was I to ruin this happy occasion for them? There must be something—anything—to be thankful for, and then I saw it.

"I am thankful for sweet potato soufflé." I smiled, satisfied with my answer. The others weren't though. Butterball looked hurt, Gabs looked shocked, and Dirk...well, Dirk looked insulted. I had hurt these people that I was sitting with. I took a deep breath and spoke from my heart.

"And I am thankful for Paisley's smile each morning, the opportunities Butterball has given to me, the rekindled friendship with Gabrielle," I said and turned to Dirk and his family. "And I am thankful for you welcoming me into your home and sharing this special dinner, as if I was family." I smiled with satisfaction. I'd done well. I thought of something to make each one of them happy, and it worked. Thanksgiving wasn't ruined.

Sweet potato soufflé was passed around, as well as turkey, stuffing, seven-layer salad, Butterball's famous, homemade rolls, dressing, and steaming giblet gravy. As each person passed the serving bowls, I watched how they interacted. Conversation flowed easily, and the laughter intermingled with talk. Colby and Cole were adorable as they stuck spoons on

140

their noses with Dirk doing the same. When his wife cleared her throat and gently reached out to touch his shoulder, his composure changed, and his eyebrows lowered, making the boys put the spoons down. His half-smile reassured them, all was still well. This was my family now, all of them. They say you can't pick your family, but they picked me…, and Paisley. I really *was* thankful for much more than sweet potato soufflé.

***

It wasn't long before Christmas decorations and ornaments decorated lawns. Pink flamingos in Santa hats, plastic-red garland strung on white picket fences, and white lights hanging from rooftops blinked in the dark of night. This would be my first Christmas in a home with a family and not a motel since my dad died.

One evening, as we filled our bellies with grub from Myra Jean's, Gabrielle started to talk about a Kris Kringle party they had planned.

"Wait a minute. Christmas is three weeks away, and I'm just now hearing about a party?"

"Well, you are hearing about it now," Gabs said as she squirted ketchup in circular designs on her fries.

"How big is this Kris Pringle party?"

"Kris Kringle. Not Pringle," Butterball corrected. "Huge. You'll love it. Plus, it's a chance to improve your photography skills and maybe get clients of your own." Butterball displayed a few of my best photos from Wakulla Springs in the house and was just itching to show them off. As comfortable as I was here, I was close to getting the money I needed to buy a used car since I had heard nothing of my dad's.

Later in the evening, Gabs went in the hallway and pulled down the stairs to the attic entrance.

"Whatcha doing?" I asked from a comfortable spot on the couch.

141

"*We* are getting the Christmas tree down. Get over here," she beckoned.

She stood on the ladder five feet above me. From the waist up, she was invisible, as a cloak of darkness from the attic covered her. All I could see was her bottom half. If it was still Thanksgiving, I would be thankful for the blue jeans she wore, as it kept me from possibly seeing another sequined thong. A few particles of dust drifted down around her as she shifted things around. If I didn't know better, I would have thought a body was being dragged across the attic floor.

"I got it!" She dragged it closer to her and tilted the end out the attic door for me to grab. I pulled slightly, and it came down, knocking me backward on my butt. The weight of the tree and its girth made it impossible to get it off, and each time I tried, I was attacked by a five-foot porcupine. Gabs rushed down the stairs and hoisted it off of me.

"Death by Christmas tree," I gasped. "What a way to go."

She laughed. "That's just the bottom half. Give me a minute." She ambled back up the ladder and brought down two more pieces in zippered bags. She unzipped and pulled them out. Each piece looked smaller than the other.

"I've never seen a dissected Christmas tree before," I said. "Dad always had real trees."

"Oh, these are the best—no needles on the floor and easy to snap together."

It took less than five minutes to piece it together, and the limbs fell open, perfectly placed with no gaps to cover with tinsel or large ornaments. Mini-white lights were already built into the tree. All we needed to do was connect the three sections and plug it into the wall.

"Presto! Instant holiday," I said. I stood back and took it all in. The lights started to blink off and on in a pattern. Like a moth to the flame, Paisley crawled to the tree, wide-eyed.

"How are we going to keep her away from the tree?" I asked as I caught her foot in the nick of time and picked her up.

"Supervision," said Butterball as she came into the room, carrying a large, clear, plastic container. Small wads of bubble wrap and old newspaper filled the container. Butterball reached in and carefully removed the bubble wrap from a white porcelain angel with a twisted gold band of a halo on top. Butterball had the entire tree to put the ornament on, but she still took almost a full minute to find just the right spot.

"Simon gave this to me on our first Christmas together. He said I was his angel with a crooked halo."

"I don't understand," I said.

She continued to stare at the ornament. "There are imperfections in *all* of us, Tess."

The room filled with the sound of Bing Crosby Christmas music that Gabs found on the radio station. I spent the better part of the afternoon, helping hang ornaments that spanned three decades, and each one had a story. Ornaments of exotic feathered birds, plastic pink flamingos, wine cork reindeers, Styrofoam candy canes, and an assortment of other treasures. Each had their place on the tree. The most unusual was an old, wooden fishing lure with small, teardrop crystals hanging from the hooks.

"What's the story behind this one?" I asked as I handed it to her, still partially wrapped in old newspaper.

"My dad was an avid fisherman in the rivers around here, and my mom was more refined, so to speak. She dealt in antique crystal," she said and laughed at the memory. "I wanted a little bit of both of them when I moved out, so I stole an old fishing lure of Dad's and did the same with a few crystals from one of Mom's old broken chandeliers she bought at a flea market to refinish." Butterball placed that one up high, away from little fingers that might be too curious.

"Oh, I almost forgot one." Gabs ran to her purse and pulled out a small, brown bag with tissue inside. She handed me the heavy wad of tissue. "You get to put the last one on. Butterball and I picked it out for you."

143

I unfolded the tissue, and my eyes fell on a beautiful, miniature snow globe with an ornate, gold base. Inside the snow globe was a picture of Paisley as she slept. An angel. She had the face of an angel. Paisley reached out to touch it, and, for once, I didn't yank something back from her touch. I found one vacant spot left on the tree and slid it on the branch in its new home. It blended perfectly with the other Mitchell family ornaments. Even though we had different last names, it sort of worked. Of all the things they'd done for us—shelter, food, a job—it took something no bigger than the palm of my hand to rattle me.

"Are you crying?" asked Butterball.

"No," I said wiping away a tear. "I'm allergic to pine trees."

"Artificial pine trees?" she asked as she Elvis Presley-bumped my hip.

"Maybe," I answered as Butterball and I simultaneously reached to put the lid on the empty plastic container. "Thank you," I whispered.

CHAPTER SEVENTEEN

A few days later, I awoke to the sound of scratching and whining at my bedroom door. Paisley stirred at the unfamiliar noise, and I quickly stumbled out of bed to see what the commotion was about. When I cracked the door to look out, a tan creature darted under the bed.

"I saw her run down the hallway. Is she in there?" Butterball asked as she shoved me aside to see for herself.

"Shh," I said as I pointed to Paisley and whispered. "Whatever it was it ran under the bed." I rubbed sleeping sand from my eyes.

She squatted beside the bed and bent down on one knee and one arm as she looked under the bed. "Come here, baby. Don't be afraid. Little ole Butterball ain't gonna hurt you."

"Was that a dog?"

Butterball sat on her haunches. "Yes. I fed it scraps on the beach because it looked skinnier than my little pinkie, and now I can't get it to go home. I tried to sneak in the house, and it ran between my legs."

"Don't tell me you don't know about stray animals. Once you feed them, they adopt you. That mutt has a home all right. It's right here."

"Ridiculous. I just need to get it outside, and it will go home," she said in denial.

It took half of last night's rotisserie chicken to get the dog from under the bed. No collar adorned its neck, and it had a skeletal body.

"Poor thing. Nobody loves you?" Butterball cooed, took her from my arms and received wet kisses.

"You know what we have to do," Butterball said, nodding her head in opposition to me shaking mine.

Thirty minutes later, Paisley, Butterball, Gabs, and I were sitting in a veterinarian's office. Butterball tried in vain to restrain the hyper puppy, but it had to have caffeine coursing through its veins instead of blood.

The front door opened, and a familiar little girl walked in with a page boy haircut. She held it open while a huge, white, shaggy-haired dog bounced in dragging Aaron.

He winked at me, signed the dog in at the counter, and took a seat next to me with Penny on the opposite side. Her eyes widened in recognition, and she took the leash from her dad, pulling her dog toward her.

"Better watch yourself, Rascal. She might spit gum in your hair, and no one will ever know you were once a sheepdog." Rascal whimpered and lowered his head.

I hung my head in shame as Aaron nudged his daughter to correct her behavior.

"That's a nice looking boxer you have there," he said as he patted her head. "I'm guessing maybe nine weeks old."

"She's a boxer?" I said.

He raised his eyebrow in question. "You bought a dog, and you don't know what kind it is?"

Butterball and Gabs laughed at his remark, and Paisley attempted to yank off her left shoe. I knew what that would lead to. I passed her off to Gabs and casually scooted forward to block his view of her toe-sucking fetish.

"She isn't my dog. Butterball found her running loose on the beach. No collar, so we're hoping the vet might recognize her."

"Ms. Mitchell, we can see your dog now," said the vet tech.

We waited ten minutes before an elderly man entered the room. He was tall, almost as tall as Aaron, mid-sixties, dark hair with touches of gray in his close-cut goatee, and sparkling blue eyes that made Butterball's eyebrows perk up. They quickly lowered as she refocused on the dog.

"Hi. I'm Vince Castellari."

He was Italian. Butterball loved Italian food.

We made simple small talk until the exam was over. The puppy was given a clean bill of health. Remarkably, no heart worms or parasites.

"She needs to put on a few pounds, but other than that, you have yourself a pretty little boxer girl," said the vet as he smiled at Butterball.

"She's not ours," I said. "She was a stray on the beach. Do you know of anyone who wants a boxer?"

"Yes, me," chimed Butterball as she smiled at the vet.

We stared at Butterball, speechless. It was Gabs who found her voice first. "Don't you think that we should take her to a shelter? I'm sure they will find her a good home."

Butterball picked the boxer up off the stainless steel table. "Look, I know we need a dog about as much as I need to start menstruating again, but I just can't put her in the shelter. I mean, look at this face." Butterball shoved the dog's face into Gabs's. Gabs reached up and wiped away the eye boogies from the dog, and her resolve weakened as her bottom lip quivered.

"This isn't fair. It's just not fair. How can you have bonded with this dog? You've just found it. No, absolutely not. Of all the things to bring home. A dog. *A dog*! Fleas, ticks, and worms. They carry *worms*, Butterball. And I ain't talking about the Worm Grunting Festival kind. I'm talking hook worms, tape worms, and ring worms. No, just no!" she said with determination as she folded her arms across her chest and stamped her foot.

***

147

One dog crate, one twenty-pound bag of dog food, and a dozen squeaky toys and doggie treats later, we made it home.

"I'm saying this once so listen closely. I am not cleaning up pee or poop," insisted an angry Gabs.

The dog ran around the house to inspect every room. She peed in the kitchen, dining room, and living room within ten minutes of getting home.

"How about Harriet," suggested Butterball as she cleaned pee for the third time. "My Aunt Harriet used to have droopy jowls, and I know as this dog gets older, she will too."

"Did you like your Aunt Harriet?" asked Gabs.

"Yes."

"Then don't," said Gabs.

"How about Penny? I heard that somewhere, and her fur is the color of a penny," offered Gabs.

"That's because it's Aaron's daughter's name," I said as I rolled my eyes.

"Oh, wipe that then," she said with a wave of her hand.

"I like Ruby," said Butterball. "Scooby with a twist."

"Ruby Doo, it is." Gabs finalized the naming of the pooch.

"Ruby, Ruby Doo, where are you?" Butterball sang out.

"She's over by the dining room table, pissing again," Gabs said between tight lips.

***

We were diligent for two weeks with the puppy, but Ruby was no closer to being potty-trained than Paisley was to walking. I cleaned up dog poop three times in one day because Butterball had a photo shoot, and Gabs was missing in action. My plans to leave resurfaced and looked better and better with each passing poop-filled day.

When I thought Ruby's bladder was as dry as the Sahara Desert, Paisley found a pee puddle and happily smacked her hand in it to entertain herself. I had another fun-filled afternoon

148

cleaning up pee and stripping Paisley down for a bath after I put Ruby in her crate.

As Paisley sat in the warm water, surrounded by bubble bath, I studied her features as I often did. Her slanted eyes, bridgeless nose, the extra space between her big toes and the next. Butterball said that when God made her, he made a true Floridian because her feet were made for flip flops. I found no humor in it.

What would she look like when she grew up? Would she have a boyfriend like the one in the mall, or was that girl the exception? Would she be able to rock climb? Heck, forget rock climbing, would she be able to just walk? I stared into her eyes, willing her to reach for the sides of the tub, pull herself to stand and say, "Hey Mom, check me out. No worries, I'll be running marathons in no time."

I concentrated so hard trying to reach those brain cells to reprogram them to my schedule and not hers that I gave myself a headache. I slid my hands under her armpits and raised her up enough so that her feet were flat on the bottom of the warm porcelain tub. I slowly started to relax my grip.

"Come on. You can do it if you will just try," I whispered.

Ruby barked loudly just as Paisley's knees buckled. I tightened my grip a mere second before she disappeared under the bubbles. I yanked her from the water, briskly dried her, and wrapped her in a towel. What was I thinking to be so careless with her? I was shaking when Gabs walked in the house.

"Whatcha been doing?" she asked.

If you only knew, I thought. "Pup sitting again. Butterball had a photo shoot, and Paisley found a pee puddle."

"Hmmp," said Gabs as she grabbed Ruby's leash and released her from the crate. "I guess since this four-legged garbage disposal is now a resident here too, I might as well take her out once in a while."

Gabs took her out to the backyard. The chickens piled on top of each other and kicked up dirt and small feathers in an

149

attempt to stay as far away from Ruby as possible. Ruby, oblivious to the drama she was causing, barked in excitement as Gabs pulled her in the direction of the beach. For someone who didn't want a dog in her house, she sure was having fun running with Ruby on the beach. Gabs stopped several times to let Ruby sniff the sand and to kiss a little girl building a sand castle.

Things just seem to come easy for Gabs. She has a great beach house, family still with her, a boyfriend, and now a dog. She's just missing a kid. The more I thought about it, the tighter I held onto Paisley.

CHAPTER EIGHTEEN

Our Kris Kringle party was something else. Food covered every inch of the kitchen countertops, including an extra folding table we borrowed from Dirk and Kara. I had never seen such a large amount of food: four hams, four turkeys, southern sweet potato soufflé, homemade macaroni and cheese, seven-layer salad, green bean casserole, stuffing, giblet gravy, deviled eggs—thanks to our backyard chickens working overtime—and an assortment of other side dishes and desserts that company brought.

I met Uncle Henry and Aunt Gladys again, and even ninety-five-year-old Aunt Meme made it. Chase Redding from The Springs came with a new girlfriend. Vince Castellari showed up and paid special attention to Butterball, which rattled her and made her blush at the same time. And Butterball's best friend, Abby Sinclair from the sheriff's office, was there. I drilled her about my car.

"Have you heard anything yet? Any leads?" I accosted her as she filled her paper plate with food. She tried to avoid looking at me by going to the other side of the counter. I persisted.

"How about the chop shops? Have y'all looked there?"

She shook her head and stuffed a cheese cracker in her mouth.

"Look at me!" I ordered as I reached out to touch her arm. Butterball intervened and pulled me away to introduce me to Gabs's boyfriend, Jack McCammon. I could see how she was attracted to him. His light brown, shoulder-length hair was pulled into a smooth ponytail at the nape of the neck. He had maybe an inch in height over Gabs, and his gray eyes focused on her. He wore khaki pants with a button-up, yellow shirt that was missing a button near the top. Loafers covered his feet. Gabs introduced him to everyone with her hand slinked over his arm. He turned in my direction, and something sparkled on his earlobe. It was a diamond stud. That had to have been Gabs's doing. She brings out the fun in people. I thought I'd met just about everyone in Crawfordville, with all the festivals and events I had taken photos of, but there were people I'd never seen.

Tall, red, tapered candles wedged in silver candleholders found a home, nestled in a string of garland stretched across the mantel. Five red stockings with white fur trim hung from brass nails embedded in the mantel. Our names, sprinkled in silver dust, were on the white trim, including one for Ruby. I kept staring at Paisley's stocking from across the room. The Christmas tree we decorated had bred a multitude of gifts since the first guest arrived.

Each time the doorbell rang, a new present went under the tree, and Ruby went berserk in the crate. You'd have thought the Tasmanian devil was trapped in the bedroom, trying to get out. It became so bad that Dirk turned the ringer off. We ended up opening the curtains and taking turns being the doorman.

We quickly moved into the kitchen to keep up with the food and mess. Things went pretty smoothly, until Gabs asked, one time too many, for Butterball to hand her something.

Butterball slammed her chunky fist on the top of the kitchen counter and grabbed both of her breasts from the sides. "Do you see milk coming out of these babies? I ain't your mama. Get it yourself!"

Gabs looked shell-shocked but gathered her wits and continued without missing a beat. "No more eggnog for you, Butterball. You're cut off."

152

Butterball stormed off in a huff when she saw Vince smiling at her again.

More and more people came in, so many that I thought they would be hanging out the windows. I was overwhelmed with the people and noise. Escaping to the bathroom and leaving the entertaining up to Gabs and Butterball was a good idea. I turned on the overhead vent to drown out the noise. I decided, while I was there, I might as well go before a line formed at the door. I settled down on the white throne to take care of business and picked up a folded newspaper left on the floor. Something black, about the size of a walnut, fell from the paper and landed between my knees. To my horror, it was a huge, black palmetto bug, which now lounged in the crotch of my undies like it was a hammock on a warm summer day. All I could think was that the thing was trying to go where only one man had gone before.

I sprang from the toilet and shoved my underwear down to my ankles in an attempt to get them off. My pants and shoes prevented them from going any further. The more I jumped and screamed, the more the roach used my undies as a trampoline. When the roach spread its black wings to fly, I completely lost it. I screamed louder than any school fire alarm I've ever heard and grabbed the newspaper to beat it to death as it landed on the shower curtain. I swung so hard that it knocked the shower rod off the wall.

"Die, just die!" I screamed as I pounded the roach into the floor. One antenna went in one direction, and a spiky leg went in another. It still wasn't dead enough for me. I continued to beat it to dust until I heard someone clear their throat behind me. I turned around to see five people in the bathroom doorway staring at me: Butterball, Gabs, two guests I met a few minutes ago, and, of course, Dirk. Since my pants were still around my ankles, I was thankful for my long shirt which covered my business.

Dirk smiled at me. "Fancy seeing you here again."

153

Butterball smacked him in the stomach, and Gabs popped him in the back of the head. Butterball and Gabs stepped in and closed the door behind them.

"Is it gone?" I asked looking around frantically. "There was a roach the size of a boulder that fell out of the newspaper as I was peeing. It landed in my underwear." I kicked off my shoes, ripped off my pants and undies, and shook them furiously to make sure no parts of the roach flew back into my underwear. I didn't care that I was naked enough to get a gynecological exam. I just knew I didn't want that roach on me.

"I told you to call the bug man, Gabrielle," Butterball fussed.

Gabs rolled her eyes. "Well, it's gone now. Put your panties on, pull them up like a big girl, wash your hands, and come help us." She turned to leave. "Maybe I can just tell our guests that you fell asleep on the toilet and had a nightmare."

"Are you kidding me?" I pointed in the direction of the living room. "I'm not going out there until everyone is gone," I said.

Butterball turned to me. "You have to. This is our *only* bathroom. Well, the only one we want the guests to use. I stopped up the one in Gabs's room this morning," she said as she looked down with guilt.

Gabs gave her a look that said, "I'll take care of you later."

"They can go down the road to Dirk and Kara's house for all I care," I cried while getting my clothes back on.

"Be reasonable here, Tess. I know you're embarrassed, but get over it. We need you in the kitchen. Come on and make yourself useful," she ordered.

"Useful," I said as if that was a new concept. "Is that all I've been these last few months? Something useful? Yeah, I guess so," I said with my hands planted on my hips as my voice elevated in pitch. "I was just that poor little girl, with a messed up baby, Butterball found in a restaurant. I'm sure Butterball was looking for a loser like me, someone who was desperate enough to come home with a complete stranger with the promise of food, shelter, and maybe a few dollars. Yeah, I looked like I would be useful enough as a temporary photographer. I was even more useful as a nurse after the surgery."

I washed my hands, but kept on talking. "Useful enough to potty train a puppy for two people who don't know the first thing about a dog." I turned around and stamped my feet. "Hell, I chicken-sat for you people!" I was on a roll and didn't know when to stop. "If my car hadn't been stolen, I'm sure I would have been useful as a taxi too. If I stay around here long enough, I'm sure I'll be useful as a babysitter for Aaron McMasters.

"Y'all don't see it, do you? I'm not useful to anyone, much less Paisley." I closed my eyes and wished away the last few years. When I opened them, Gabs and Butterball were still in the bathroom, staring at me. Tears started to roll down my face. "I don't know how I got to this place in my life. Did I tell you that when I was still in Alabama, I got wind that Social Services were getting ready to take Paisley away from me?" I nodded my head. "I didn't let them. I left, but the funny thing is I didn't do it for her. I did it because I didn't want to be alone. Not that I loved her or couldn't bear my life without her and all that mommy mushy stuff, but for one simple, selfish reason. I didn't want to be alone. I don't know how to take care of her, which is obvious. I'm selfish, and, as strange as this sounds, since I dragged her from one state to another, I want nothing more than to be alone right now."

Snot dripped on my arm from my nostrils, and I wiped it away. "Those are your friends out there, not mine. They're all being nice, but I know it's because I'm staying with you. I mean, seriously, who would befriend someone like me? Even Aaron's daughter can see the real me. I mean, the girl had two feet of her hair amputated because of me. Her hair," I screamed and grabbed my own to prove my point.

155

I was hysterical, but I couldn't stop. It was like watching an uncapped blender slinging batter and not reaching over to hit the off button or yank the cord from the wall. The words just kept coming like lava.

"And, do you know that I considered chiseling the meg tooth from the fireplace and hocking it for money? Yep. That is the kind of person you let in your house, Gabrielle. That is the kind of person you let take care of your *chickens*," I hissed. My shoulders sagged from exhaustion after the outburst of emotion.

I didn't wait for a response. I stormed out of the bathroom right into the middle of everyone standing there in silence as "Grandma Got Run Over by a Reindeer" blared from the radio in the background. The guests heard every single word of my fanatical rant. Ruby whimpered and hid behind the couch when I looked at her. I tried to rush past a couple of people and came face-to-face with Aaron. Penny stood next to him with a vice grip on his thigh. Paisley was in his arms. He handed her to me with no words. He looked wounded, and I hung my head in shame as Gabs and Butterball emerged behind me.

Penny broke the silence. "Daddy."

"Yes, pumpkin?"

"Ruby ate something."

He smiled at her. "I'm sure she ate a lot of things today. Everyone has been giving her snacks."

"No, Daddy. She doesn't look right, and she is making funny burping sounds."

I was glad for the distraction. Aaron went to Ruby and took to one knee to examine her. When he pressed on her belly, she whimpered, and he heard a faint, muffled beep.

"Butterball, do you still have that old metal detector in your closet you told me about?" he asked.

"You don't think—" Butterball didn't finish her sentence as she disappeared into her room and reemerged, holding her metal detector.

156

She held the wiggling pup down as Aaron scanned her belly. We all heard the metal detector beep loudly.

"There's gold in them there bowels," yelled a tipsy guest.

"It doesn't surprise me. That dog will eat anything," said Butterball. "I've seen rainbow-colored poop in the backyard. I still haven't figured out what's missing to give her rainbow-colored poop."

Vince Castellari came over to check Ruby out. He felt her abdomen and spoke to her in baby talk. I could see Butterball's face soften a bit.

"Whatever it is, it's too big for her to pass. I can feel it. Bring her to my office, and we'll get it out. I'll meet you there." He said this to no one in particular, but within three minutes Gabs, Butterball, Aaron, Penny, and I were in the car following Vince. We left the other guests in the care of Dirk and Kara to entertain.

CHAPTER NINETEEN

We piled into the waiting room of the vet's office. Vince picked up the wiggling pup. "I'll take her back and get x-rays. It will be a few minutes." He disappeared into the back room with her.

I wanted to just get in my car and drive away, far, far away from all of this. But I didn't have a car anymore. Hell, I was ready to take a bus. I just didn't care. How was I ever going to face everyone when we went back to the house? I picked up the latest issue of *Mutts Need Love* and buried my face in articles about doggie nail polish and minty-breath treats to get rid of doggie breath. Everyone else paced the floor, but I kept my eyes focused on the pages. Maybe, just maybe, no one would confront me about what happened. Not only did I feel awful about it, but I felt awful that I felt glad Ruby ate something. The focus was on her, at least for now.

Minutes later, Vince called us into the room to view the x-rays. We saw the outline of Butterball's key chain, with five, separate keys in Ruby's stomach.

"She'll be here a while as I prep her for surgery. You all can go back to the party if you want, and I'll call when she is ready to be picked up." Nobody moved a muscle. "Okay. Make yourselves comfortable. This will be a while."

As we walked to the lobby, Vince called to Butterball.

"Naomi, do you get sick at the sight of blood?" he asked.

"No."

"I usually have an assistant here with me. I don't want to call anyone in since it's a holiday. Do you mind just handing me the tools?"

Butterball paused as if to decline. "Sure. I guess I have to make sure we get all the keys, right?" She smiled and disappeared into the back room with Vince.

On the day we should be celebrating the birth of Jesus, we celebrated the birth of Butterball's keys, by cesarean so to speak. A few minutes later, more people from the party appeared in the lobby of the vet's office. We stayed there for two hours, yet it seemed more like three days. Vince finally appeared and said all was good as he held up Butterball's keys in a clear, plastic bag. Butterball smiled in her pale, green garb and hair net.

Guests lingered around talking. I didn't know what to say after my episode in the bathroom. I looked around at these people who'd left a party to check on this puppy. I learned that they thought she was mine and pitched in enough money to cover the vet bill. Who does that? It had to have cost over a thousand dollars. Were there really people out there like this? I didn't know if I would have done the same if the tables had been turned.

During my two-hour wait, I thought a lot about what I said at the party. Funny how all those words came out easily, but taking them back was like swallowing a brick whole. I thought of what I said about Aaron and Penny and turned to look for them. Gabs told me they left, once they found out Ruby was okay. That dreaded conversation would have to wait for another day.

Finally, we took a partially conscious Ruby home. Dirk and Kara had already cleaned the kitchen, put the leftovers in the refrigerator, while their boys entertained Paisley. We placed Ruby in her crate and sat down to eat at the dining room table.

I heard the heat kick on, and the silence was deafening. No clinking of glasses, shuffling of feet, conversations followed by

159

laughter, or the occasionally loud greeting as someone new came in from the cold, nothing. What I thought was too much, I actually missed now. Presents still surrounded the trunk of the tree.

"I completely forgotten about the presents with all that we just went through," I said.

Butterball walked to the tree with a cold turkey sandwich in one hand. "Well, what are you waiting for?" She and Gabrielle rifled through the presents as I settled on the couch with Dirk, Kara, and Paisley. "Tess, you should come see this." She waved me over.

The first gift, wrapped in red with gold-sparkled ribbon, was for me. The next one, covered with silver-striped ribbon, was tagged for Paisley. I plundered through several gifts.

"They are all for me and Paisley," I said, dumbstruck, my mouth hanging open like a baby bird waiting to be fed.

Butterball was excited. If she'd been a balloon and I stuck her with a pin, she'd have shot all around the room.

"Well, hurry up. They aren't going to open themselves."

Dirk excused himself and took some trash outside, while I started to open the gifts, with Paisley on the floor beside me. Butterball took pictures. Twenty-one gifts, and each one of them contained cash, various amounts of twenties, fifties, and even several hundreds. They could have taken all their money back after my outburst, but they didn't.

"I can't accept all this." I reached for a tag to see who brought it. There were two words, either "To Tess" or "To Paisley." There was no way to return the money. I was excited and frustrated at the same time. There was enough here to get a decent used car. I could leave! Why was it again that I wanted to leave? Gabs and Butterball hadn't really asked any more from me than if I was family. If anything, I'd used them. I'd eaten here free, hadn't paid rent, and learned a trade in photography.

160

"I owe all of y'all an apology." I stared at the floor, too ashamed to make eye contact after all I'd said. "I behaved awful today." I shook my head. "No, not just today, but from the beginning, all the way back to when I first met Dirk at the gas station. I've said some terrible things and hurt many people."

"Oh, we knew you weren't all that and a buttered biscuit," Butterball teased.

The crying started. "I can't believe it took all this to get me to see that you truly care about me and Paisley. I just didn't feel deserving of it, I guess. I'd put up such a wall. I'm surprised anyone got through."

Dirk came to me and patted me on the back. "Hey, kid, don't worry about it. I was twenty times worse than you growing up. But Kara found me, and everything changed."

Kara rolled her eyes. "You're still messed up, but I tolerate you," she teased as she rose from the couch. "We need to get home. It's been a long day for the boys and us."

Dirk opened the door before us and stood there, staring at the driveway. "What is that?" We looked around him at a pristine, restored Thunderbird.

CHAPTER TWENTY

Blood rushed through my veins so fast I could hear my heart beat in my ears. I squealed as loud as I did on Christmas when I was thirteen, and Daddy bought me a ten-speed bike, but this was much better than a ten-speed. I hugged everyone, even Dirk.

No rust, no dings, no paint flaking like a ten-day-old sunburn. The teal, glossy paint was so shiny it blinded me. The old, squeaky hinges that groaned when I opened the driver's door were now silent. I even had a new roof, minus the duct tape. The new teal-leather seat behind the steering wheel felt great. The leather was smooth, not brittle and dry rotted. I looked up into the rearview mirror at everyone still standing near the porch and smiling. When I turned around to wave at them, I saw a present sitting solo in the middle of the back seat.

The wrapping was different than any of the other classic Christmas gifts. Cartoonish worms wearing top hats and dancing with canes covered the wrapping paper. The tag said, "From Aaron and Penny."

The black-leather photograph album was soft to the touch. Embroidered in calligraphy across the middle in silver thread was, "The Memory Collector." Five photos were inside: one of Butterball, Gabs, and me cooking in the kitchen; one of me and Paisley at the beach, building a sand castle; Paisley hand feeding the chickens a small cherry tomato with a huge grin on her face; Ruby and Paisley snuggling together asleep; and the last one made me laugh out loud. It was taken from a distance at the Worm Grunting Festival. It was a picture of me falling face first into Aaron's arms with his hands cupping my cheeks as I stared up at him. Someone in the crowd, obviously thought this was a moment to capture and did so.

On the inside cover, Aaron had written, "To new treasured photos and memories – Love, Aaron and Penny." Right below that was a wheat penny. It was taped to the inside cover with an additional note that said, "For luck."

I was dumbfounded. This was a dream. Nothing this good ever happened to me. My rearview-mirror-family was still smiling at me. I carried the album in my hands and returned to them.

"Hey, think about it. You don't need to buy a new car now, do you?" said Butterball.

That thought hadn't crossed my mind yet. I had all this money and a car too.

"What are you going to do with the moola?" Gabs asked.

"I think she is a bit overwhelmed," Kara said with concern in her eyes.

Overwhelmed was an understatement. I sat on the porch steps to pull myself together. I hung my head between my knees and took deep breathes. I had a car, but I needed a job to keep gas in it. I had a place to live. Okay, time to grow up fast, Tess. Think, think.

I felt the weight of Gabs's hand on my knee as she braced herself and sat down beside me. "I know what you are thinking. You and Paisley are welcome to stay here as long as you want. I don't remember the last time I've had this much fun. Besides, I need a girlfriend around here." Butterball huffed at that comment, and Gabs blew her a kiss.

"Think of your future," Gabs started. "You and Paisley could always—"

"I want to go to college." The words burst out of my mouth in one rush of air, surprising myself as well as them. "I never finished high school, so I'm not sure how to do this." I couldn't

163

believe I was actually in a position to consider college as an option.

"I have friends who work at the Adult Education Facility in Tallahassee. That's where you get your GED. You'll need that before enrolling in college. I can give them a call and see what you have to do," offered Butterball.

I shook my head. "Thanks, Butterball, but I need to do this on my own." I rose from the steps. Butterball had begun to cry.

"I didn't mean to hurt your feelings."

"No, that's not it." She sniffed and wiped her nose on her forearm. "My little Tessie Coop is all grown up," she wailed.

Dirk took that as a sign that it was time to leave. He took Kara's hand in his and walked away with their boys. I made it to him before they reached the end of the driveway.

"I guess I can assume my car wasn't really stolen," I teased. "You did this, didn't you?"

The deep lines in his face stretched and curved as he smiled. "I had some help. Your Thunderbird helped a bunch of high school kids in mechanics class to earn an A."

He was quite surprised when I slammed my body against his and squeezed with all my might, my face against his chest. I caught a whiff of the same kind of cologne Dad used, mingled with an old cigar. I'd never been close enough to Dirk to notice it. It was actually comforting.

"I can't pay you back right away. It will take time," I said.

"You plan on being here a few years, right?" he asked with a stoic face.

I braced myself. "Yes."

"You like our boys, right?"

"Ah, I see," I smiled. "This isn't a fair trade though. Babysit your sweet boys in exchange for a complete restoration of my dad's car?"

"You're right. It isn't a fair trade, but those two sweet boys are going to grow up into hormonal teenagers. Get ready." He laughed a good belly-roll of a laugh.

164

Despite myself, I gave him another hug.

CHAPTER TWENTY-ONE

After supper the next evening, I tried to swallow the lump that formed in my throat as I called Aaron. Penny answered the phone. "Hello?"

I swallowed hard. "Is Aaron home?" I asked in my most cheerful, staged voice.

"Maybe." Her voice bristled when she heard mine.

"If I promise never, ever, ever, ever, ever to chew bubble gum around you again, may I please speak with him?" Begging was not beneath me.

The longest pause in history followed, and then she answered. "That includes jaw breakers, lollipops, and anything else sticky. Do I make myself perfectly clear?"

"Yes, ma'am," I said, hoping she couldn't hear my smile.

The phone clattered down on a table, and the sound of shoes running away from the phone faded.

A moment later, he picked up the receiver. "Hello?"

"Hi."

"How's Ruby?" Concern touched his voice when he recognized mine.

"Ruby is doing great. We had to go back this morning and get a cone on her head, so she wouldn't lick the stitches. If you place her in just the right spot in the yard, you can get stations from overseas on the television."

He laughed. Thank goodness he liked my stupid joke.

"I hear you have your dad's car back. It wasn't stolen after all?"

"Dirk isn't what I thought he was," I said.

"People surprise the hell out of me too," he said, and for a moment I wasn't sure if he was saying that figuratively, or if it was directed at me.

"I've made some decisions…decisions that will affect me and Paisley."

"I'm glad. I wish the best for you, Tess," he said, as if ending the conversation. My heart sped up. I couldn't let it end this way. I didn't want a boyfriend, but I didn't want one less friend either.

"I'm going to stay here and go to college. I'll be staying with Gabs until I'm done and can find a place of my own. I have my own clientele, thanks to Butterball. I'll do okay if referrals keep coming in.

"Good." After all that, that's all he had to say?

"Thank you for the gift," I said.

"You're welcome. I wanted to give it to you in person, but well, you know what happened. It was a crazy day with Ruby and all." He was being nice, but distant.

I stood there twisting the phone cord around my finger until it constricted and became an anaconda, squeezing the life out of my finger.

"I know I was childish, and I hurt a lot of people at the party." The anaconda squeezed tighter. "I'm not good at apologizing, because I've always thought I was right. Well, lately, I've been wrong. Actually, I'm sure it hasn't been just lately, but for the sake of moving this conversation along, I'll just say I've been wrong about a lot of things."

He was silent, so I continued.

"I came here with Paisley trying to run from my past." I paused and thought of Paisley. "But it's impossible to escape what you're running from when you bring it with you. Now, I'm not sure what I would be running from anymore if I left here." I took a deep breath and stretched my tense neck muscles. "I think I've reached the finish line here. I don't know if I won or not."

"But you're going to be brave in the attempt," he added.

"What?"

"It is part of the Special Olympics oath. You probably don't know about that yet, but you will."

"I just want to say I'm sorry, and thank you for the gift you put in my car," I finished.

"You're welcome." There was that awkward silence again, as if he was waiting for more from me. Time to spill the beans.

"I've never really shared my past with you. I never knew my mom. She died during my birth. The day I left Brooksville, Alabama, was the same day I attended my dad's funeral. There was nothing there for me anymore. Paisley's dad was a high school mistake, but Paisley wasn't. He denied she was his and left on an athletic scholarship. I was an ugly, dark stain in his life and to those at high school. Gabs moved away before she knew I was pregnant and before my dad died of cancer. After my dad's funeral, I just climbed in the car with Paisley and hit the road.

"Aside from Paisley, the things I brought with me as reminders of my previous life were an old coin I no longer have and my dad's photo album. It contained the memories I wanted: two photos of my mom, one of her and Dad's wedding, and one with her pregnant with me. It was full of other pictures of me growing up that Dad had put in it. The day he was diagnosed with cancer, I quit putting pictures in it. I didn't want those memories." A deep, ragged breath escaped. "I don't have any of Paisley in there, as I hadn't accepted that she would be part of my memories, at least not any good ones.

"When I made those comments in the bathroom to Butterball and Gabs, I had just reached a very low point in my life. I was angry, embarrassed, and lashed out at them—and you, indirectly—then the chaos with Ruby began. When I saw the present you gave me, it made me think about all that I have here. I found my best friend from high school again, met a woman who treats me like her daughter, and people who genuinely care about me and Paisley. I even met this decent guy at the Worm Grunting Festival." I heard the springs on a bed decompressing as he laughed.

"Although, I think I messed that one up when I spat bubble gum in his daughter's hair."

"You got that right," whispered Penny, a tad too loud in the receiver.

"Hang up the phone, Penny." I heard a loud click. "I'm still here," he said.

"I came down here thinking my baggage was Paisley, but it was really my attitude. The album you gave me opened my eyes. You gave me something no one else had. Butterball, Gabs, and you gave me good memories again and the possibility of future ones. I'm finally putting down some roots. I've found my home." I started to cry. I was sick of crying all the time.

"Tess," he said.

"Yes?"

"Women sure do talk a lot."

"Yes, we do," I chuckled. "I'm not looking for a relationship. I just—"

"Let me tell you something," he said with authority. Oh no, this was it. I just didn't know when to shut my mouth. No man wants to hear your life story. Another one bites the dust.

"Tess."

"Yes?" A lump formed in my throat.

"I have a story too. Last year on the anniversary of my divorce, I was in the mall in Tallahassee. I was coming down the escalator and glanced out into the crowd when I was struck in the head with a wheat penny. A wheat penny! Probably a penny someone attempted to toss into the fountain to get a wish fulfilled. Someone's wish wouldn't come true. I had stolen it by accident. The penny bounced two steps down from me. I barely grabbed it before it went under the step. I ended up by the

169

fountain, debating about throwing it in for the poor soul who tried before me, but I didn't. I'd heard that wheat pennies are rare and they can bring a person good luck. That's why I put it in your album, Tess, just maybe, you could use a little bit of luck in your life. Do you believe in luck, or do you think things just happen in random acts, like dominos falling down?"

I was breathless. That was my dad's penny. I was sure of it. Maybe with it falling into his hands, my wish was granted. I wished for laughter and happiness, and I'd had both of those mixed in with tears.

"How about you and Paisley come over tomorrow at about noon for burgers and fries."

"Sounds good. We'll see you then." And then we hung up.

CHAPTER TWENTY-TWO

I strolled into the living room, smiling, thinking of the wheat penny. Gabs placed an empty Christmas box on the couch.

"What are you smiling about?" she asked.

"Burgers and fries at Aaron's tomorrow."

"Ah," she said as she packed up Christmas decorations. She dropped a napkin ring, and I watched as it rolled under the coffee table. I bent over to pick it up.

"You're wearing it!" she shouted.

"Wearing what?" I answered as I shot up straight as an arrow.

"Wearing what, wearing what," she mimicked with a smile. "You know what. The zebra-striped thong." Her eyes were wild looking.

"Don't be ridiculous. Only a harlot would wear trashy stuff like that," I lied and turned my back to her to gather more Christmas decorations.

"I know what I saw. Unless you are sporting a new sparkly tattoo across your tushie top, then you're wearing it," she insisted as she came for me with her fingers in a pincher grasp. I turned to run, but with the strength of an Amazon warrior, she grabbed the back of my jeans at the waist band and threw me face down on the couch, pounced on my butt, and straddled me. I half expected her to start swinging her arm in the air and yelling, "Ride 'em cowboy," but then I felt the thong being pulled back and released with a loud pop that stung my upper backside. I cried and laughed at the same time and begged her to stop. Then she began to sing, "It ain't wrong to be wearing a thong, all night long, and act like King Kong."

"That makes no sense," I said as I laughed. I struggled to get up as she continued popping.

"It doesn't have to make sense. It rhymes." She laughed, and then she was silent and all popping stopped. She grabbed me by the shoulder. "Tess, look."

I turned my head away from the back of the couch to look in the other direction. I saw Paisley standing there. Standing there! Not holding onto anything. We both held our breaths, afraid to move or make a sound. As if that wasn't enough, she did the unthinkable. She took three steps all by herself before she fell on her padded butt. In excitement, I bucked Gabs off my back, tossing her off the couch. We both ran for Paisley. We made such a commotion that Butterball came running out of the bathroom with shampoo still in her hair, holding her bathrobe closed.

"What the hell is going on? Are we getting robbed?" she yelled as she sputtered, the shampoo dripping off her face.

"She's walking!" Gabs and I said in unison.

"Bout time, too. She needs to earn her keep. Get her to take Ruby for a walk later," she said with a smile as she returned to the bathroom. I heard a loud "yippee" from behind the closed door.

"Gabs, this is going to be a great year! I can feel it." I squeezed Paisley until a burp came out.

"You just need to take it day by day. Paisley will take it step by step, and it will all fall into place."

I thought of what the waitress at Myra Jean's said when she caught Paisley snacking on her toes. "You know what, Gabs. Toes make great appetizers," I said with a wink, ready for the main course.

"The Special Olympics track and field will be the main course." She winked back. "I'll make the banner." We laughed.

CHAPTER TWENTY-THREE

My meeting with the counselor at the Adult Education Facility went well. To everyone's surprise, especially my own, I was considering the nursing field. Butterball and Gabs were pleased, but as nice as it was to get their approval, I was doing this for Paisley's and my future. Butterball survived with me taking care of her, so I must have some skill.

Butterball came home from grocery shopping with a large envelope containing our Christmas, New Year's celebration, and other various photographs. I ripped the package open. They were the best photos I'd ever taken, if I did say so myself. I filled my new photo album with these treasures. It was filled with pictures from Christmas, my new car, Butterball cleaning the chicken coop, Gabs modeling my new thong over her blue jeans, Paisley walking in the kitchen, hallway, living room, bedroom, bathroom, and driveway. Rock climbing would be next at the Worm Grunting Festival. Well, maybe.

I put the last two in. One was of Penny teaching Paisley patty cake, and the other was of Aaron blowing a huge bubble from his gum near Penny's hair as she screamed.

One can never have too many friends. If Aaron and I were never anything more than friends, it was just fine with me. I was just starting to get my life straight for Paisley and myself. A good friend was all I needed. After all, this was the beginning of me.

***

The following Saturday, I took my first solo road trip in my dad's renovated car. The leather seats were warm as I drove with the top down. My hair was a tangled mess after the drive on the interstate. It was a long, quiet drive and gave me time to think of what I needed to say to rectify a bad parting with Dad. I slowed to a crawl at the entrance of Goodbread Plantation. I hadn't planned on ever seeing those iron gates again, but they hung open, welcoming me in.

I parked the car a few feet from my parents' burial plot. I rehearsed what I'd say on the drive up, but nothing sounded right. People were walking around the cemetery, taking photos of loved ones' graves, and, on the far side, a burial was taking place. The car became stifling since there was no breeze to cool me down.

My feet took over, and, without thinking, I found myself holding flowers in front of their graves. They fit perfectly in the small, built-in vase attached to the concrete slab. They were just a simple handful of wildflowers I'd pulled out of the median about three streets away, but they worked. The freshly raised sod had taken root and was blending with older grass that surrounded the newly placed concrete top. It would take time to depress like the rest—like Mom's—but it would, one day. Dad's engraving still looked fresh, while Mom's was covered with algae. My fingernail scraped the crud from her name. I didn't know her, but Dad did, and that was good enough for me. I wiped my green-coated fingers on my jeans, inadvertently pushing it underneath my fingernails to the quick. I picked at the thin line of algae under my nails in procrastination of what to say. How do you apologize to someone, who isn't alive anymore, for something awful you said in their presence? It didn't matter that he couldn't hear me when I said it. The problem was, I said it when I really didn't mean it. They can't hug you and say, "It's okay. All is forgiven." What could I possibly say to make up for the words I'd said when I left?

I pictured myself with teenaged Paisley, arguing over clothes, food, and what she could and couldn't watch on television. Maybe we would have the same arguments that Dad and I had. I hoped so.

I reached out to touch his name as I had done when I'd left long ago, and as I touched the engraving, a warm sensation rippled through my fingertips, flowed through my forearm, and into my heart. And the words flowed easily. "I love you."

About The Author

    Zelle Andrews's first endeavor at writing was at the age of twelve. A short poem she wrote in middle school was selected to be published in the *Tallahassee Democrat*. Later in life, she found the yellowed newspaper clipping that her mother had saved.

    Paisley Memories started out as an idea Zelle wrote on a scrap piece of paper. Just notes at first, then it became a couple of chapters. It was her first Tallahassee Writers Association conference that made her take her writing seriously. The novel evolved over the next four years and found a home with Southern Yellow Pine Publishing.

    Zelle Andrews lives near the Florida coast with her family. She is a member of Tallahassee Writers Association. *Paisley Memories* is her debut novel.

CPSIA information can be obtained
at www.ICGtesting.com
Printed in the USA
FSOW01n1713281216
28901FS

9 781940 869544